# MATS AND ME

WAVES Flight Attendants on

Navy Transport Aircraft

by Billye Grymwade

Published by Puma Press
116 Blackburn Place
Ventura, California 93004-1255

Copyright © 2003 by Billye B. Grymwade

Prepared for printing by Mehle Printing, Inc.
2250 Craig Drive
P.O. Box 6157
Oxnard, California 93031-6157
www.mehleprinting.com

Cover Design by Penny Henschel

ISBN: 0-9742649-0-3

Printed in the United States of America

October 2003

10 9 8 7 6 5 4 3 2 1

# DEDICATION

*To all my Navy flight attendant shipmates from VR-3:*
*Keep on flying*

# ACKNOWLEDGMENTS

To my Mentor No. 1, Mr. Tor Welch, I extend my gratefulness for his editing services and for pushing me into the sometimes murky world of self-publishing.

To my Mentor No. 2, Josette Dermody Wingo, I express my gratitude for her invaluable suggestions and arrangements in the world of book marketing.

To my fellow WAVES National members of the Channel Islands Unit #20, I give thanks for their brainstorming input for this book's title.

# PROLOGUE

"The pigeons are walking, but NATS is flying." So the saying went in the Naval Air Transport Service during and after World War II.

VR-3 (Air Transport Squadron THREE), one of several NATS squadrons, served in many different capacities from March 1943 through 1945: it conducted a Multi-Engine Plane Commander School and a Multi-Engine Co-Pilot School; operated R4D (2-engine aircraft) air evacuation flights, complete with litter setups (instead of seats) and onboard corpsmen; flew weekly flights to Montreal, Canada, with flag stops in Ottawa; flew a schedule of four flights per day, coast-to-coast; and flew a transcontinental Hospital Flight schedule, six flights per week.

In 1946. VR-3 was moved from NAS (Naval Air Station) Olathe, Kansas, to NAS Patuxent River, Maryland. The squadron used the 2-engine R4D as well as the 4-engine R5D. At Patuxent (familiarly called "Pax"), VR-3 continued to fly cross-country. Some flights were non-stop, often referred to as "The Hotshot," between Maryland and California. Other flights were also cross-country, but with an RON (Remain Overnight) at NAS Corpus Christi, Texas. That flight was named "The U-Route."

At the close of WWII in 1945, many men and women were discharged from the military services. VR-3, along with all the other VRs, was losing most of its male flight attendants. Word was spread throughout the Navy that enlisted WAVES (Women Accepted for Voluntary Emergency Service), who were not being discharged from the Navy, were invited to apply for flight attendant duty.

A 10-day course was established in the late summer of 1946 at VR-3, NAS Patuxent River, Maryland, to train those women to be Navy flight attendants (flight orderlies was an earlier designation). Upon completion of that course, the WAVES were assigned to the various VRs throughout the Navy's aviation arm.

In 1948, Navy equipment, crews, and base facilities of NATS were combined with the Air Force's ATC (Air Transport Command). At that point, the organization became MATS (Military Air Transport Service). On 1 January 1966, MATS was replaced by MAC (Military Airlift Command). Navy squadrons were not included in MAC; it was an Air Force entity exclusively.

In mid-1948 VR-3 became a feeder line for the Berlin Air Lift. The flights went from Pax to Washington, D.C. (deecee), to Westover AFB (Air Force Base) in Massachusetts, to Stephenville, Newfoundland, and to an AFB at Lagens (now known as Lajes) on the island of Terceira in the Azores (islands in the Atlantic Ocean, which belonged to Portugal).

After a minimum of 14 hours' rest in the Azores, the crew continued on to England, Germany, Morocco, or Iceland. Once in a while, there would be a flag stop at Orly Field in Paris. Occasional shorter VR-3 flights went from Pax to Hamilton AFB, Bermuda.

Using the smaller aircraft, the R4D, VR-3 also performed daily flights (Monday through Friday) to go from Pax to NAS Willow Grove, Pennsylvania, to Harrisburg, Pennsylvania, and return to Pax. Those flights, called "The Ruptured Duck" or "The Hernia Special," were mainly cargo runs, providing cargo for further shipment by the larger aircraft in the squadron.

VR-3 was the last of the squadrons to be decommissioned. That was in 1967. During the great years of NATS and MATS, pilots, co-pilots, navigators, aviation mechs, radiomen, male hospital corpsmen, Navy nurses, and male flight attendants comprised the crews. Then there were WAVES flight attendants. They also flew.

# BOOK ONE

1946 - 1949

# Chapter One

Jean Trimwood was of medium height, looking good in her uniform, with rich chestnut brown hair, and arresting blue-green eyes. She was born in 1920 in Tempe, Arizona. At age 22, in 1942, she enlisted in the Navy. She had completed four years of college, majoring in math, a minor in home economics.

It was Jean's intention, upon enlisting, to "work" in the Navy, rather than "manage" or "administer." With her math schooling, she was assigned to a Navy storekeeper's school in Milledgeville, Georgia. Upon completion of that school, she was assigned duty at a Navy disbursing office in Cleveland. She transferred to VR-3 for the flight attendant school in the summer of 1946.

The squadron's routes were the "Hotshot," and the "U" Route. At the onset of the Berlin Airlift in 1948, the squadron's mission was changed. Jean had a flight with a male flight attendant. By then, only a few male flight attendants were left in VR-3.

Preparations for beginning a flight included the pilots' and mech's making a visual check of the exterior of the plane. The radiomen were aboard. Meanwhile, Jean and her partner distributed the blankets, put pillow cases on the pillows, put paper head covers on the tops of seatbacks, and made a count of first-aid equipment and ditching equipment and signed for all of it. The last things to come aboard were food: the lunch boxes or Maxson Meals and cans of soup; and urns of beverages—coffee, milk, and water.

The first leg of the flight, from Patuxent River to deecee, was very short, approximately 15-20 minutes, chock-to-chock. The crew then waited in the deecee terminal before takeoff time. Jean noticed an RAF officer seated by himself at a table in the snack bar.

She went over to him and said, "Are you alone, Commander? And have I used the right rank?"

"Yes, and yes," he replied as he looked up. *Cheeky lot, these American women!*

"I hope you don't think me to be cheeky, approaching you this way," she said.

He turned red in the face and said, "Well, as a matter of fact, I was thinking exactly that! But I assure you, I've already changed my mind, quickly, about American women. How charming, what you did. Won't you join me?" He stood up, pushing back his chair, then pulling out the chair next to his in an easy, fluid motion. She sat in the proffered chair.

"Thank you, Commander. And I *did* address you with the correct rank? Right?"

"Close. I'm Wing Commander Reid, RAF. And it's 'W/Cdr' on your passenger manifest, with my name, Michael Reid. And you are?"

"Oh, just call me Jean. Last name's too unusual in America and too common, probably, in England."

"And what does all that mean?"

She explained. "My roots are in England. There are probably countless relatives in London, let alone all of England. I hope my flight out of the Azores goes there. I want to take the train to London and look up my surname in the phone book."

"Then, I wish you good luck."

"Thanks. Well, my flight partner just gave me the sign to get back on board. You going on this flight?"

"I believe so."

"See you on board, Commander."

"Righto."

Later, as he reached the top of the ladder, she greeted him with "Welcome aboard, Commander Reid." She noticed how uncommonly tall he was. Slim. Angular. She guessed that he would have difficulty fitting himself into one of the aircraft's seats. She thought, *can't do anything about that now.*

He nodded and smiled, in a friendly way, not guarded, and entered the main cabin, ducking his head.

\* \* \*

The plane landed in the Azores, and the crew debarked. The passengers, with a fresh crew, departed for England after a two-hour stay in the Azores.

At the end of Jean's crew's rest time in the Azores, plus a part of another day, she was delighted to learn that their next flight was going to England, just as she had hoped.

Upon arrival at the Burtonwood USAFB in England, and dropping off her flight bag at the Nurses' Quarters (there were no separate accommodations for enlisted WAVES), she took a station bus to the main gate.

She carried a musette bag with food that she had purchased in Maryland. It contained a large canned ham, canned vegetables, canned fruit, crackers, tuna fish, some sugar, and various other and smaller items. From the main gate, she took a cab to the railway station and boarded the train for London.

The train ride into the city was pleasant enough, everything being so new to her. In London, her phone-book search proved to be fruitful: she found four Trimwoods in it. She called the first one listed, thinking she might as well be systematic about it. She waited, a little breathlessly, while the phone rang.

In that first phone call, she talked to Mrs. Agatha Trimwood, wife of Donald Trimwood. Jean explained who she was, how come she was in England—and London—and why she was calling: to see if Mr. Trimwood might be a relative of some sort.

Agatha was delighted to know that a possible relative from America had called, so she invited Jean to come to the house and wait for Donny to come home from work.

Jean asked, "How do I get to your house? I'm at the Victoria Station."

Aggie gave her the instructions, and an hour later, Jean was at the doorstep. Aggie, upon seeing the uniform, knew it must be the American woman who had called. She threw her arms around her to hug her warmly and invited her in. Aggie was a sturdily built Englishwoman, graying hair, a pert smile for everyone.

Jean was a bit overwhelmed with the greeting, hearing all her life that the British are so stiff, cool, aloof. Never mind, she thought; exceptions for everything.

As soon as she entered, she placed the musette bag on a chair and said, "Mrs. Trimwood—"

"Oh, dearie, you must call me Aggie."

"Aggie it is. Thank you. Aggie, I've brought you some foodstuffs. See if there's anything you like. You can have it all, of course."

Aggie peered into the bag and spotted the canned ham first. "Upon my word, Jean, this is very magnanimous of you. So much food! A package of sugar? No, *two* packages of sugar!" She continued the search and said, "This is a real treasure! Dearie, how can we ever thank you for such generosity? And you must stay for dinner. We'll have a virtual feast!"

At that moment, someone came down the steps from the second floor. A gentleman dressed casually in slacks, an understated polo shirt, and knock-about shoes. Tall. Nice-looking.

He got almost to the bottom step when he said, "Jean? Is that you?"

Jean looked at Aggie, as she wondered who that could be, calling her by her name.

Aggie said, "It's my brother." Addressing him, she said, "Come here, Michael, and meet Miss Trimwood. . . . Wait a minute. You called her Jean. Do you know her?"

Michael nodded to his sister briefly, then spoke to Jean. "Is this the household you were looking for? My brother-in-law is your relative?" *Look at that lovely chestnut brown hair. Fabulous!*

"Commander Reid! What a strange coincidence! When Mr. Trimwood comes home, we hope to compare ancestry notes and see if we are really related." *Mmm mmm. Look at that gorgeous blond hair. Fabulous!*

"Upon my word," he said, "imagine meeting you again, like this, in my sister's house!"

"Weird, huh?" she exclaimed.

Michael drew closer and searched her face. *And those eyes. Blue? Green? No, I think blue-green. Fascinating!* He then said, "Weird, yes. Also wonderful, yes!"

She looked him in the eye and thought, *Man oh man, just look at those dreamy gray eyes. Fascinating!* Aloud, she said, "Oh, yes, I think it's wonderful, too."

Michael turned his attention to his sister, saying, "Aggie, dear, Miss Trimwood was a flight attendant on the first leg of my flight back to England. She is staying for dinner, isn't she?"

"Of course! I'll make tarts for dessert. Haven't had tarts in such a long time."

\* \* \*

When Donald Trimwood came home, he was eager to meet the American visitor. Aggie had already phoned him about Jean.

He was a civil servant and dressed the part, wearing a conservative dark suit and tie, white shirt, plain black shoes, black socks. Like Aggie, his hair was graying, a charming man, and ever-so polite.

At dinner, Donny and Jean discussed what they knew about their family members—who went to America and when. In the end, they deduced that their great-grandfathers were brothers.

So," she said, "what about the other three Trimwoods in the London phone book?"

Donny answered, "They're all my brothers. Got two sisters, too. Both married. They're in the book, different names, of course."

"That makes us shirttail relatives, doesn't it?" Jean asked.

Donny said, "One might also say, 'kissing cousins.'" Whereupon he leaned toward her, around the table's corner from him, and planted a cousinly kiss upon her cheek.

Jean was surprised, but pleased, as well. *No stiff, cold Englishmen here!* Her thought was loud and clear.

Aggie beamed. Michael smiled. He touched the napkin to the corners of his mouth, pushed back his chair, and said, "Come, Jean. I want to show you the neighborhood."

"Oh, Commander, I couldn't do that. I should stay to help Aggie with the dishes, wash or dry, put them away, sweep the floor, wipe off the stove……"

"Nonsense!" cried Aggie. "Go along, the two of you. Donny will help me do all that, won't you, dearie?"

Donny nodded and smiled all the way to the kitchen.

* * *

When Jean and Michael stepped outside, they discovered that the streets and buildings were concealed by a thick fog. They began to walk.

Jean thought, *Fog! Oh, well, that's usual for London, so I hear.*

Michael said, "Do not be alarmed about the fog, Jean. Fog is usual for London."

She stopped in her tracks. He stopped also and looked back at her. "What is it? Forget something?"

"We did it again!"

"Did what?"

She said, "Remember in the terminal in Washington? You thought I was cheeky, and the next thing I said was something about *being* cheeky. Well, we just did it again. Only in reverse. As soon as we stepped outside the house, I said to myself that fog is usual for London. Then, for heaven's sake, you said aloud that fog is usual in London."

"Two minds on the same track?"

"I guess so!"

At the next corner, Michael paused and opened a door. "In here, my dear cousin-in-law." They entered a small pub, noisy and smokey. They sat in a booth toward the back. "Two ales, please," he said to the waitress.

"Oh, Commander, no ale for me. I don't drink alcohol."

"Incredible!" Then he called to the waitress, "Miss, make that two sodas instead."

"Oh, Sir, you don't need to change your order!"

"Not a problem, my dear Jean. How come you don't drink?"

"Two reasons. First, religious, you might say. Second, health. It seems that with each sip of alcohol, some brain cells are destroyed."

"That might make me reform!" They laughed together.

Jean said, "So, Commander, . . ."

"Jean, dear. Please stop calling me 'Commander.' I know, it's part of the officer/enlisted protocol. But I feel that since we're related, so to speak, by marriage, you should call me Michael."

"Oh, I'd love that . . . Michael."

"And what were you about to say?"

"I was wondering . . . don't you have to report somewhere, upon returning to England?"

"Oh, yes, and I've already done that. Now I'm on leave."

"I see. Well, . . . Michael . . . and that's going to take some getting used to. I was also wondering about something else. What did you do in the War?"

At this point, Michael gave her a brief history of his adult life. He entered the Royal Air Force in 1940, at age 22. He had studied law in an English university, but Britain's pressing need for pilots was so great that he got "drafted" into flight training.

"Flew bombers, mostly," he said. Went down over Germany, got captured, lived in a Stalag until repatriation at the end of the War. Then I spent some months in hospital."

"Were you wounded?"

He waited a beat. Then continued, "You might say so."

"Good heavens, were you tortured?"

"What an imagination! Well, yes, there was that. But not overmuch. Just enough to give me the hospital time, once I returned to England." *And to meet Winifred . . . and to fall hopelessly in love.* "Well, Jean, shall we return to the house?"

"Whatever you say, Comman . . . I mean Michael."

"That's the girl."

When they emerged from the pub, the fog seemed to be worse. Jean was concerned about getting back to the base and was quite sure there would not even be a flight scheduled.

She said to him, "I think I'd better say goodbye to Aggie and Donny and get back to the base and see what the schedules look like."

He understood her concern, having had so many pilot hours in the air, himself. He said to her, "There's a call box up ahead. I'll connect with your base for you, and you ask Operations about it."

When she had finished the phone call, she announced, "There's bad weather that's come down from Iceland. All flights in and out of all Europe are canceled."

He asked, "Were you given a time to return to base?"

"Yes. Operations said not for two more days! Good heavens! What on earth am I supposed to do for two days?"

"I'll tell you. First, we'll go home and tell Aggie and Donny of your change in plans, and then we'll invite you to stay over at the house. I am inviting you now. You can have my room, and I'll sleep on the couch."

"Ah, Michael. I couldn't do that! Take your own bed?"

"Nonsense, dear. Besides, I read half the night, and that would interfere with your proper sleep and rest, if *you* were on the couch."

"Michael, you're so sweet."

He was mildly startled. He hadn't been told that for a long time. *Not since Winifred . . . not since just before Winifred married a colonel in the British Army.*

When they arrived back at the house and Michael told Aggie and Donny about the turn of events, Aggie immediately invited Jean to stay with them.

Jean said, "Michael has already made that invitation."

Aggie said to herself, *So it's Michael, now. Well!*

Jean then said, "I believe I'll turn in now. Been a long day. Thank you for the neighborhood walk, Michael."

He nodded with a smile and said, "Good night, Cousin Jean."

With a smile on her face, Jean followed Aggie upstairs. Aggie showed her Michael's room and the bathroom and her bathroom linens. Jean washed up, brushed her teeth (most flight attendants carried a collapsible toothbrush and a sample-size toothpaste tube in the bottom of their purses), washed out her underwear, put on a nightgown borrowed from Aggie, and went to bed. *I'm lying in his bed. I'm lying in his bed. I'm lying . . . So? What's the big deal? I'm lying in his . . .* Sleep attacked her immediately.

* * *

The next morning after breakfast, Michael took Jean on a circuitous tour of London, in spite of the fog. They took the underground here, a bus there, a cab now and then, and walked a lot. They did the London Tower, Westminster Abby, a river boat ride past Big Ben, and they walked across London Bridge. They had lunch in a pub near Kensington Gardens. He showed her the Saint James Palace, Clarendon House, and Buckingham Palace during the changing of the guards.

They returned to the house at dinnertime. Aggie was in the middle of cooking with her newly acquired pantry items Jean had brought. After dinner, Jean suppressed a yawn, and she announced that she was exhausted and would retire. "Have to be fresh when I go back to the base tomorrow."

She turned to Michael and offered her right hand, saying, "I don't know how I can thank you, Michael, for such a wonderful day. You took me to so many places. Knowing that my ancestors hailed from here, I felt as though I had come 'home.'"

He took Jean's hand and squeezed it unusually hard, more than he had intended. To make up for the gruffness of his handshake, he put his other hand on top of hers and stroked it gently. "In a way," he said, "you *have* come home."

She liked that thought.

Jean said goodnight to the others and climbed the steps. She washed up and brushed her teeth, washed out her underwear and put on the borrowed nightgown again.

She did not fall asleep immediately as she had told the others she probably would. Again she began thinking about Michael.

*Silly goose! Stop thinking unthinkable things about this stuffy Englishman! But he's not stuffy. Not really. He's... quite nice. Quite nice, indeed. Stop it! Silly goose!*

Aggie and Donny had retired early, and Michael, having bathed and changed into pajamas and robe and slippers, settled down in his chair with a book. About two hours later, he heard footsteps on the stairway. He looked up. There, coming down the steps, was Jean in her utility coat, wearing Aggie's nightgown underneath.

He got up and met her at the bottom step. "Anything wrong Jean?"

"No. I mean yes. I can't sleep."

"You said after dinner that you were so tired . . ."

"I know what I said. But I was wrong. I couldn't sleep for thinking about you, Michael. Oh! There I go, being cheeky again! Forgive me."

"Not cheeky," he said. "A wonderful euphemism is 'straightforward.' Don't change that, Jean. It's too endearing for words. Come, let's sit on the couch, and we'll talk until you get sleepy."

"I don't want to interfere with your reading," she said.

"That won't happen. Not when I can have a congenial conversation with someone like you." They sat down onto the couch. "Actually, I haven't made much sense with my reading, anyway. I've been thinking about you, too. About us."

She said, "I don't think I know exactly what you mean."

"Perhaps," he said, "this will clarify what I mean."

He put an arm around her shoulders.

*That feels really nice,* she thought.

He tilted her face upward, leaned downward, and kissed her lightly on the lips.

She responded. "Oh, yes," she said. "That clarifies things a bit."

"Well," he went on to say, "I intend to clarify things a lot!" And this time he kissed her more passionately.

Afterwards, she took a deep breath and said, "I do see what you mean now, but I'd love some more clarification."

They kissed once more, his hand moving down to her thigh.

She broke off and jumped up from the couch. "That's it," she said. "No more. It's getting out of control! I can't afford to let things get out of control, Michael. I mean it!"

He took her hand nearest him gently. "I know that, and you were wise to break off. I had the most dishonorable intentions imaginable! But, Jean, dearest, I promise it won't happen again. Please. Sit down. Let's talk."

\* \* \*

When Aggie came downstairs in the morning at 6:00, she was startled to see her brother and Jean sitting together on the couch, fast asleep. He had one arm around her shoulders. Her head was resting against him. They were both fully dressed, in nightwear.

*I wonder . . .* she thought. "Naw!" she said in a light whisper.

\* \* \*

Michael, back in uniform, accompanied Jean for their journey by train to the Burtonwood USAF base. He said goodbye to her at the bottom of the steps leading to the Nurses' Quarters. He told her, "I've been wanting to tell you something these last two days."

"Like what?"

"I may get a transfer to Washington. Soon."

"Deecee?"

"I beg your pardon?"

She explained, "Washington, District of Columbia, or deecee."

"Yes! Of course!" He smiled as he thought about it. He went on to say, "I've just recently completed training and orientation for military attaché duty. The orientation part was my being sent to Washington. Seems as though the law schooling I've had is coming in handy after all."

She grasped both his hands. "Michael! That's wonderful! I can't wait for that to happen! I'm so happy to hear that kind of news."

"And I'm happy to hear *that*!"

Then, a U.S. Air Force nurse stepped out of the main door to the nurses' quarters and took one look at the two people at the bottom step. She gave Jean a disapproving stare as she went down the steps and walked haughtily to the bus stop, ignoring the wing commander altogether. The bus pulled up just as she arrived there. She got on board.

Jean and Michael watched her go. They looked at each other. In unison, they said, "Tommy Rot!" Then they laughed, sharing another moment of thinking the same thing and even saying the same thing together.

Then they sobered. "Oh, Michael," she said. "I can't wait for that transfer to take place. I hope it really happens!"

"Nor can I wait for it to happen. Sweet Jean."

They kissed a long and endearing kiss, and then she was up the steps and into the building.

\* \* \*

When Michael returned to the house, Aggie was waiting up for him. It was late. She said, "Michael, I need to ask you a rather important question."

"And what would that be, my good sister?" he asked.

"Michael, my dear brother. Have you forgotten Winifred yet?"

"No, not yet, Aggie. I don't think I'll ever forget her." He sighed. "But I can safely say I've gotten *over* her." He looked downward and said, "I must have gotten over her because . . . "

"Because?"

"Because I've found someone else. I didn't think I would ever find someone else to take the place in my heart that Winifred held for so long." *I still remember the day I met her at the hospital. She was an angel of mercy in a nurse's uniform.*

Aggie sat back in her chair and smiled, saying, "I thought as much!" She regarded him for awhile, listening to his silence, and said, "And I'm glad for you, dear brother."

He looked at her and smiled.

*The dear boy*, Aggie said to herself.

\* \* \*

Jean spent the flight back to the Azores, and the next flight back to Pax River, in a daze. She couldn't believe what she had just experienced. She couldn't hope any more nor any harder that Michael's transfer would become a reality. She was on Cloud Nine whether she was aloft in the aircraft or walking on the ground.

"Hi, there, Shirley," Jean called out, upon entering the quarterdeck. She put her flight bag down on the deck.

Shirley Jackson was the MAA (Master at Arms) for the WAVES Barracks. She had attended college for two years on athletic scholarships. Then she worked for one year in the recreation department in St. Louis. She had reported to the first regiment of the boot camp for WAVES in July 1942 at age 21. After boot camp, she was assigned to a Master-at-Arms job in the WAVES Barracks at NAS Olathe, Kansas. In late 1945, she was transferred to NAS Patuxent River, Maryland.

Shirley said, "Oh, hi, Jean. Have a good flight?"

"The best!"

Helen Enasevich, with ash blond hair and soulful brown eyes, entered from the lower-deck wing of the barracks with the green flight bag in hand and set it down next to the desk/counter of the MAA office.

She said to Jean, "The best what?"

"The best flight ever!"

Helen, teasing, said, "Something really grand must've happened!"

"Oh, it did." Jean looked at the visitor waiting in the lounge, just off the quarterdeck. "Isn't that Ensign DelMar sitting in there?"

"Oh, yeah," Shirley offered. "Waiting for Elizabeth. Who else?"

Jean and Helen nodded, and, rolling their eyes, said, together, "We know. We know."

Elizabeth Holmes was one-of-a-kind: short, petite, whitish-blonde hair, bright, china-blue eyes, and with a personality that would not quit. Men adored her. She, in turn, seemed to adore each one equally.

Wearing her lipstick straight across her upper lip, without a cupid's bow, was a trademark unique to her. Her shipmates thought it was an affectation—possibly from San Francisco, her home town.

Jean said, "Want me to get Elizabeth, Shirl?"

"Not necessary. She already knows Ensign DelMar is here."

"Okay."

Ginny Gray appeared from the second deck. She had brown hair and brown eyes and was of medium height. Fair skin completed the benign description of her. She knew she was plain. She was from New Mexico. She hoped, when she entered the Navy, that her home state would add some sparkle to her history. So far, no such luck, she noticed.

Ginny greeted Jean with, "How did your flight go?"

"Absolutely dreamy!"

"What's so dreamy about a flight?" asked Ginny.

"Yeah," Helen chimed in. "Give."

Jean instructed them, "Listen to this. All of you. I'm going to tell you a story that'll make you so envious!"

She proceeded to tell most of her London experience. They listened with genuine interest. Shirley took in all of it, too.

Then Jean left to do a shower before going to evening chow. Helen's bus transportation arrived to take her to the terminal, and she waved goodbye to Shirley. As she passed through the door and reached the first step, she spoke to Lt. Albertson. "Good evening, Lieutenant."

"Good evening....Helen, isn't it?" He seemed to remember having her on some previous flight.

"Right! Excuse me, Lieutenant," Helen said. "I've got to board the crew's bus. It's waiting for me."

"Sure, Helen. Have a good flight."

"Thanks. I will."

Lieutenant Albertson strode purposefully up the steps to the WAVES Barracks. He was a tall, rangy Midwesterner from Iowa, 29 years old. He had shiny blue-black hair with clear blue eyes. He received a Navy Reserve commission in 1942, at age 23, having completed four years of college and one year working in a bank. After pilot training in a Navy flight school, he flew Navy transport aircraft exclusively. Today, he hoped to meet up with Elizabeth Holmes. He kept missing any and all connections with her!

He pulled open the door just as Elizabeth and Ensign DelMar approached to leave the building. DelMar said, "Hello, there, Lt. . . . ."

"Albertson," he filled in for him. "Frank?" he said to Ensign DelMar. "You two going out together?"

Ens. Frank DelMar smiled broadly and said, "You bet!" And off they went together. Down the steps Elizabeth went and out of Lt. Albertson's life, again.

He entered the quarterdeck anyway, and stalked up to the MAA desk. "Damnation!" he shouted at Shirley. "It's happened again!"

"I know what you mean, Lieutenant. You almost missed her altogether." Shirley remembered that Lt. Albertson had, in the past, made numerous phone calls, trying to reach Elizabeth, as well as trying to hook up with her at the barracks.

"Doesn't matter," he said. "I still don't get to go out with her, ever! She's always on a flight or going out with somebody else! Damn!"

"I don't know what to say, Lieutenant, except, I'm sorry, I guess." She felt her end of the conversation was genuinely unhelpful.

"Yeah, well, sorry doesn't cut it for me!"

"I'm sorry," she said again, lamely.

"Oh, wait a minute," James Albertson said apologetically. "I had no business taking my disappointment out on you. *I'm* the one who's sorry. Really, I am. Forgive me?"

"Well, of course, Lieutenant. And shall I say, 'Better luck next time?'"

"Hmph! Gonna need *something* to get a date with Elizabeth Holmes!"

Shirley looked him in the eye and asked, "Ever think about dating someone else?"

"Not really."

Lt. Albertson left abruptly, absolutely thinking about what the MAA had just said, and thinking she may be right.

# Chapter Two

Gloria Thomas was a flight attendant assigned to VR-3 at NAS Patuxent River, Maryland. She was a real-live southern belle, born in New York City, in 1921, and taken to Atlanta to live when she was an infant. Upon graduation from high school, Gloria began working as a nurse's aide in an Atlanta hospital. She worked there for three years.

She was a honey blonde with blue eyes, pert nose, generous lips, and a firm chin. She was short and small-framed but sturdy enough for the rigors of her new assignment. Gloria had enlisted in the Navy at the age of 21 in 1942, among the first WAVES in existence. With her nurse's aide background, she was trained, in the Navy, to be a pharmacist's mate (later to be called a hospital corpsman). After that training, she was transferred to serve at the Naval Hospital, Great Lakes, Illinois.

When Gloria reported to VR-3 for flight attendant school, in 1946, she was 25 years old. Each of her first two check-out flights in VR-3 was with a male flight attendant who was a veteran member of the squadron.

In 1948 Gloria had a flight out of the Azores, which, after the required crew's rest, was ultimately destined for Frankfurt, Germany.

Two hours into the flight to Germany, Gloria noticed an Army GI, a Sergeant, using a burp bag (the paper bag conveniently stored in the back of the seat in front of the passenger). She immediately went aft and stirred up a concoction of some cool water, two drops of essence of peppermint, and a bit of sugar. It was something her father had given her whenever she had a tummy ache and felt nauseated. She gave it to the Sergeant, and he asked, "What is this?"

"Drink it," she replied. "It'll make you feel bettah."

The Sergeant took a sip, tasting it, and then finished it off. "Oh, my," he sighed. "That was great! I feel better already. What is it? I ask again."

She explained what the drink was, and he sighed again. "Thanks a lot, Miss....?"

"Thomas," she answered. "Gloria Thomas."

"Well, thank you again, Glorious Gloria!"

They smiled at each other.

He settled back into his seat and wondered, *What in the world is going on here? She was so nice....and helpful....to me, a negro. And, she is obviously a woman from the south. I can't believe it!*

\* \* \*

When they reached Frankfurt, everyone debarked from the aircraft. Gloria approached the Sergeant, not knowing his name. It had been impossible to discern which sergeant was which. She asked, "Whe-ah do you go from he-ah, Sahgeant?"

"From here," he answered, "I catch a bus outside the terminal for Wiesbaden. That's where I'm stationed. And where are you headed for?"

"Ah go to Bad Soden on a bus that takes the crew to the hotel whe-ah all the crew membahs stay foh thei-uh rest, befo-ah the next flaght out."

She continued with, "And Ah don't know yo-ah name yet."

"I'm Sergeant Virgil Blake, U.S. Army. Regular. And my work is in the Signal Corps."

"How do you do, Virgil." A dangerous(?), no, adventurous thought entered her head. She said, "Why don't you hitch a ride on ou-ah bus and come to Bad Soden with us?"

"An excellent idea!" Checking his bag in a locker at the terminal, he joined Gloria and her co-crew members. At Bad Soden, she told him she'd check into the hotel and freshen up and would meet him in an hour.

Sergeant Virgil Blake, born and raised in Toledo, Ohio, had enlisted in the regular Army at the age of 17. It was June 1942. He served in the South Pacific until 1945. After a 30-day furlough, and a refresher course in communications, he was transferred to Germany, his current duty station.

He walked through the small German tourist town, deciding what parts to see with Gloria when he would meet her later. When she joined him, she had changed from her flying uniform of Navy slacks to a Navy skirt. He thought she was quite attractive in uniform. They walked to the spa, which had dried up during the war; therefore tourists no longer came to taste the waters. The town's small businesses struggled to endure the difficult times.

They strolled through a small park, watching children who played there. They walked past Bad Soden's small and ancient train station. They poked their heads into a clock shop. Its walls were completely covered with clocks that began striking the hour. It was cacophonous. They exited quickly!

They had lunch at the enlisted men's mess—a restaurant at a banquet hall in Bad Soden. The restaurant had a U.S. military contract to feed military personnel. It also had one claim to fame: it was located directly across the street from the birthplace of Mendelssohn.

At lunch Virgil explained to Gloria why he had gone to the States while stationed in Germany. His mother was seriously ill, and he had been granted emergency leave to visit her.

"Ah'm sorry, Virgil, that yo' mamma is so sick."

"Thanks. I hated leaving her, you know. But my furlough was just about ended."

She reached across the table and put her hand on his. He patted her hand in return, looked her in the eyes, then looked away. The moment, whatever it meant, had quietly slipped away. He wondered where all this was going.

He ventured a sticky question, asking her, "So, tell me something, Gloria. How come a beautiful southern woman like you, with that magnificent southern accent, is being so nice, so friendly, with me—a negro, a colored man?"

"We-ell, Virgil. You gotta know that Ah was born in New Yahk City, and...."

He interrupted with "You're kidding!"

"Oh, no," she answered. "But while Ah was a baby, we moved to Atlanta. And even though Ah grew up theh-ah, Ah took on all my parents' attitudes and opinions.

"Foh example, in New Yahk, they hobnobbed with a lot of different kinds of people—whites, yellows, browns, reds, and coloreds. A lot of them wuh ahtists: musicians, poets, paintuhs, writuhs, ahchitects...."

He interjected with, "Architecture is an art?"

"Yes, indeed, Virgil. Ahchitectchuh deals with hah-mony and balance. It's an aht, like music, paintin' and poetry."

"I see. Please go on."

"So," she said, "besides all those kinds o' people wuh engineeus, scientists, doctuhs, lawyuhs, and businessmen—lots o' businessmen. And when mah parents went south, they continued to mix with the same kinds o' people as they did in New Yahk—coloreds included. Oh, they got called 'niggah luvahs'...a lot! But they didn't ca-uh. They wuh open-minded, even about the closed-minded people."

"And so then," he said, "you picked up on their style?"

"Ah reckon Ah did! Talkin' to you on the ai-uhplane and in the terminal was no big deal. 'Cept, meetin' you was and *is* a big deal. A really big deal, Virgil. I wouldn't have missed meeting you for the whole wuhld!"

"I feel the same way, Gloria. You can imagine, with your growing up in the south, what a big deal it is for *me*!"

"Ah take that as a compliment. Thank you from the bottom of mah haht, Virgil."

They regarded each other's faces for many seconds and studied each other's eyes deeply.

After a significant pause in conversation, Virgil began again. "So. You had colored help at home?"

"Oh, yes, Leota, and huh husband, Rollie."

"Do they eat in the kitchen?" As soon as he asked that, he regretted doing it. But she replied immediately.

"Of co-uss they do! 'Cept when my parents have company where coloreds ah among the guests. Then Leota and Rollie eat in the dine-in' room along with everybody else. Mamma and Leota do the servin', and the kid—me—eats in the kitchen!"

They laughed easily. Then Virgil asked, "Rollie a nickname?"

"No," she replied. "One day his muh-thuh heard the story of Suh Waltuh Raleigh. She liked the story so much, she named huh first son after him. She spelled it 'Rollie' 'cause she didn't know the 'Raleigh' spellin'."

She continued. "Ah miss them a lot. They crahed when Ah left for the Navy. Leota writes me every month Ah'm gone, fillin' me in on the gossip of the guhls Ah knew back home. Rollie always adds a note—the same note: 'Take ca-uh yo-self and be good.' Ah miss them so much. They ah like family, to be shu-uh."

He thought about what she had just told him. He understood the relationship, somewhat, but not completely. That's what comes from being a negro and growing up in the north.

Upon her third yawn, Virgil realized she had not rested since their arrival in Frankfurt. He asked her when did she last sleep.

"Ah had a two-hou-ah sleep period in the middle of the naght."

"No wonder you're yawning. Back we go to the hotel."

"Yes, suh!"

"Please, Gloria, do not 'Sir' me. I'm only an enlisted man."

"You-ah still a gentleman in mah book!"

He smiled a little, outwardly; he smiled hugely, inwardly.

At the bottom step of the entrance to her hotel, she took his right hand and shook it and said, "Ah can't tell you, Virgil, how much Ah enjoyed ou-ah little walk through Bad Soden. And ouah lunch. Thank you very much."

"And thank you for joining me."

He paused and began again. "I've given you my address and phone numbers—work and barracks—at Wiesbaden. Call me next time you come to Germany. I'll get a pass to meet you. And write to me, too. I fully intend to write to you." Their handshake had ended, but then he held her right hand in both of his. "I look forward with happy anticipation to see you again, you know?"

"Yes, Virgil, and Ah do, too."

"Goodbye, Glorious Gloria."
"Goodbye, de-ah Virgil."

\* \* \*

Upon her return to Pax in late afternoon, Gloria entered the quarterdeck of the WAVES Barracks and called to the MAA, "Hiya, Shirl."

Shirley replied, "Hiya, Glore. How was your trip?"

"Great, honey, really great!"

Ginny Gray, the New Mexico "plain" young woman came down the ladder with her green flight bag.

Ginny greeted Gloria. "Hey, Gloria, how was your flight?"

"Real nah-ce! Ah met someone."

"Tell me about it when I return. I'm heading out right now. Was the someone a 'him'?"

"Yes it was, and yes, Ah will tell you all about it when you get back. That is, if Ah'm not already gone on another flaght."

"Okay. Bye."

"Bye, now."

Shirley said to Gloria. "Your bunk is in the cubicle next to Elizabeth Holmes, isn't it?"

"Shuh 'nuf, Hon."

"Well, would you tell her that Lieutenant (j.g.) Connors just called and said that he'll be here in 15 minutes and could she be ready to leave as soon as he arrives?"

"I shuh-uh will, Shirl."

"Thanks."

Gloria trudged up the ladder with her green flight bag, found Elizabeth, and delivered the message to her.

Elizabeth clasped her hands and purred, "Oh, the lieutenant is so-o-o-o cute!"

She hurried out of the cubicle.

Gloria thought, *Guh-rate. Just great!*

When Elizabeth arrived on the quarterdeck, Lt. (j.g.) Connors was already waiting, having arrived eagerly—and earlier than he thought he would. They left together and caught a station bus for the main gate. A taxi waited for them there. They went to Rue's Roost, a popular hangout for naval personnel from the base.

Five minutes later, Lt. Albertson arrived at the barracks. Addressing the MAA, he asked, "Is Elizabeth Holmes here? I checked the flight schedules, and I determined she's not on a flight today."

"That's right, Lieutenant, but you just missed her," said the MAA.

"I did? My timing was off, wasn't it?"

"Seems that way."

An uncomfortable silence lay between them.

"Well," he said finally, "I guess I'll be on my way."

He hesitated and asked, "You do have a name?"

"Master-at-Arms Shirley Jackson, Sir." She gave him a smart salute even though it wasn't required by Navy custom nor regulations, indoors, nor when uncovered.

He returned the salute.

"Well, so long, Miss Jackson."

"Sir, I'm called Shirley by everyone."

"So long, Shirley-by-everyone!" She smiled at him. He was already grinning back at her. He left the quarterdeck and left the building.

\* \* \*

On Gloria's next flight, she was ready to leave the Azores and then learned that her crew was assigned to the next flight, which was headed for Germany. Her eagerness to see Virgil began in earnest. While the crew waited in the terminal for the aircraft to be prepared for the next leg, to Frankfurt, she was amazed at not what she saw but whom she saw. It was Sgt. Blake! She approached him with "Sahgeant! Whatevah ah you doin' heah?"

Just then the crew was notified to go on board.

Virgil said to her, "I'll tell you after we get airborne."

"Ah'll come straight to yo-ah seat, Virgil, as soon as Ah finish mah pap-uh work."

After the plane reached cruising altitude, Gloria did the required paper work (three copies of everything—passenger manifest, cargo manifest, and mail manifest). Then she went to Virgil's aisle seat. She leaned toward him and said, "What's up, Hon?"

"I have bad news, Gloria. My mother passed away, and I got another emergency furlough to go to her funeral. It's over. It's all over." His eyes watered.

"Oh, Honey, Ah'm so sorry. Ah feel for you, Virgil. I really do. And Ah hope that in time, this sadness will pass."

"Thanks. For that."

She squeezed his shoulder, then left him to get back to her duties. Each time she passed his seat, she gave him a guarded smile. And each time, he returned it.

\* \* \*

At the terminal in Frankfurt, Gloria turned in her paperwork to the terminal's passenger clerk. Virgil had to return immediately to Wiesbaden because he was returning on the very last day of his second emergency furlough.

After the crew's rest at Bad Soden, the crew was informed that the next flight coming into Frankfurt was delayed in the Azores for an entire day because of mechanical problems.

Gloria called Virgil in Wiesbaden to tell him the good news, but he said, "Honey, I can't get a pass so soon after coming off a second emergency leave. Darn it!"

"Ah wish Ah could see you, even for five minutes, Virgil. I just love bein' with you."

"That is so sweet, Gloria. I wish for five . . ." he thought for a moment . . . "five days to be with you, honey."

\* \* \*

Their correspondence flourished, each letter becoming more intimate, sharing thoughts and feelings.

Two flights later, Gloria, to her happy amazement, drew another flight to Germany out of the Azores. Arriving at Frankfurt, Gloria turned in her paperwork, and when she headed for the crew's bus, there was Virgil, grinning widely at her.

"Mah goodness! Virgil! Whe-ah did you come from?"

"It's miraculous," he said. "I'm on a weekend pass to Frankfurt, saw a Navy plane landing, and hurried over here on the slim chance you'd be on it."

He took her hand in both of his and said, "Must be magic for me. Magic for us."

"Well, Ah nevah!" Gloria was so glad to see him and so glad about the coincidence of his being here in the terminal, just waiting for her, that she spontaneously hugged him. He, of course, hugged her, as well.

He said,"Tell you what. You go on to Bad Soden and clean up and change uniforms and then you take the train to Frankfurt, and I'll meet you there. We'll do the town!"

"Yes, Ah remembah the Bad Soden train station."

He gave her a train schedule and said, "Only one train route out of Bad Soden to Frankfurt, but there're several trains a day. I'll meet you in the Frankfurt station. May be a stop in Horst, on the way."

She was ecstatic. She gave him another hug. He returned the hug, feeling somewhat taken aback by it all.

At the hotel lobby in Bad Soden, the plane commander, Lt. Comdr. Smithson, pulled Gloria aside and said to her quietly, "Gloria, this may be none of my business, but I saw you talking to the nigger, and *hugging* him, back at the terminal! I really think you ought not to mix with niggers. It doesn't look good."

"Commandah," she said, "Sahgeant Blake is a gentleman, an upstandin' citizen, and a patriot! I guarantee you there's nothin' untoward goin' on. And you ah raht, it *is* none of you-ah business. Sir!" For a moment, she lost her accent.

* * *

Virgil was there, at the train station in Frankfurt, just as he said he would be. Gloria almost told him what the plane commander had said to her earlier but decided against it. No sense in stirring up troubled feelings for Virgil. She was upset enough for both of them.

They took a taxi from the train station to the Red Cross Canteen where they had a breakfast of sorts. They then took a taxi tour of the city. They passed whole city blocks of rubble. The rubble had been swept off the streets and sidewalks and simply piled up in the middle of the blocks.

She asked Virgil, "Do you evah get used to seeing this?"

"Never," he replied.

At the edges of the piles of rubble and next to the sidewalks, enterprising German men and women set up shops with a piece of tin for the front, another piece of tin for the roof, and a piece of discarded plywood for a door. The wall of rubble provided the back wall of the shop. For them, business was as usual. For Gloria and Virgil, it was a sight to see with total wonderment at the dogged attempts to survive.

Then they passed a line of rosy-cheeked children. Rosy-cheeked from the cold more than anything else. Their faces were chapped. They carried tin buckets, to get their daily rations of milk. An occasional pregnant woman stood in line with them, as did an odd lactating mother. They, along with the children, were the only ones entitled to the milk dole.

Eventually the taxi stopped in front of a plain-looking apartment building. It seems that Virgil, with his text-book German, had arranged with the taxi driver to rent the driver's one-room apartment for a few hours.

When Gloria found out that, she balked, vociferously. "Whoa, the-ah, Virgil. Ah don't think Ah ought to do this, no-uh do I *want* to do this!"

He replied, "Look, I remember that first time we met, and afterwards in Bad Soden, how sleepy you got from having only a short rest during the over-night flight. So, you can take a nap on the couch, and I'll massage your neck 'til you fall asleep. No funny business, I promise. This respite is just for you. You'll feel better after your nap. Guaranteed!"

He took her hand and led her into the building and into the taxi driver's apartment. It was small but uncluttered. Actually cozy.

She was almost asleep on her feet—the train ride, the breakfast, the taxi ride—it all took its toll. She removed her purse, utility coat, jacket, hat, and shoes. Virgil had removed his great coat and overseas cap, putting them on a chair beside the sofa, and sat at that end of the sofa. She lay down with her head in his lap, and he began the massage. She fell asleep instantly.

When she awoke five hours later, Virgil's great coat had been placed over her for warmth. Her head was still in his lap, his right arm over her two arms across her waist, his left hand cradling her head at the left side. His chin was resting on his chest. He was sound asleep.

She stirred. His eyes opened. He smiled.

"You awake?" she asked.

"And hungry as a bear!" he said. "Let's go eat!"

He shook out his great coat and put it on, and he put on his overseas cap. She slipped on her shoes, donned her jacket and utility coat and hat. She picked up her purse and shouldered it.

At the opened door, she pushed it to being nearly closed, and she kissed him. He kissed her back.

"Thanks," she breathed.

"For what?" he asked.

"Foah everything . . . foah not . . ."

"For not taking advantage of you?"

Without looking at him, she said, "Yes. You kept yo-ah promise. Thank you, Virgil."

Then he put his arms around her and kissed her. She put her arms around him, and she kissed him back, this time with greater fervor.

They ended the kiss. They dropped their arms. They left the apartment.

They returned to the American Red Cross Canteen for something that passed for supper. Military personnel in Germany in those times were not permitted to eat at commercial cafes and restaurants—only the Red Cross canteens, or in military mess halls, or in a military-contracted eating establishment.

After they finished their "supper," Virgil accompanied Gloria on the train back to Bad Soden and then walked her to her hotel. They had held hands on the train, saying little or nothing. They were content just to be touching one another.

Gloria was very comfortable with that. She thought, *I can't believe I actually kissed a colored man! I hope he wasn't totally out-of-his-gourd surprised, nor turned completely off by it. But he kissed me back! I can't believe what I've been through with this dear boy.*

Virgil was amazed and ecstatic. He thought, *I can't believe what has happened to me! This southern white woman actually kissed me! She even initiated it, back at the apartment . . . she actually initiated it! The world must be coming to an end. I swear!*

When they reached Bad Soden, it was enveloped in fog. They walked, arms linked, slowly to her hotel, picking their way off the curbs, across the streets, and onto the curbs, the post-war street lamps not yet functioning. They reached the bottom step of the hotel entrance. He took her face in his hands and kissed her once more. Placing her hands on his shoulders, she responded with a sweet passion that surprised her.

It surprised him also. They kissed some more.

"Thank you, dah-lin', foah everything. Foah bein' a real gentleman. Foah bein' a great kissah!"

He smiled through the foggy darkness. "You are such a sweet person, Gloria. I . . . I . . ."

"What you try'n to say, Hon?"

He seemed preoccupied, then said in a rush, "Gloria, I love you with all my heart."

She breathed a small sigh. "I was wishin' you'd say that, you know? 'Cause I love you, too, Virgil dah-lin'. I didn't want to sound fohwahd by sayin' it first."

They stood there for long moments, holding hands again. Finally, she said, "What we gonna do, dah-lin'?"

He took a deep breath. "I don't know, sweetheart. I just don't know. We have to think about it and think about it a lot. But remember this, my darling: I love you with all the tenderness I can muster up, and I hope I never let you down."

"That'll nevah happen, Virgil."

"I swear it, Gloria. I swear I'll never let you down. I can hardly wait for your next flight to Germany—to see you again, darling."

"Ah know what you mean, Virgil, only . . ."

"Only what?" he asked with some trepidation.

"It's only that Ah'm afraid to fly."

"Good grief, Gloria. Then why *do* you fly?"

"Well, the new Navy assignment sounded excitin', and the flaght pay is great. But one day Ah added up all the big things that can go wrong on an aircraft that I know about, and to that Ah added all the little things to go wrong that Ah *don't* know about! And then I got real scared . . . afraid to fly."

He held her hands tightly. "You know you can go off flight status, any time."

"Yes, Hon, Ah know that. But that'd mean Ah wouldn't get to see you anymo-uh. And Ah just can't make that kind of tradeoff."

They kissed passionately once more. She broke away, quickly, and said, "I bett-uh go in, Honey. G'night, Dah-lin' Virgil."

"Good night, dear one, my Glorious Gloria, and have lots of sweet dreams."

She ran up the steps and through the double doors. She was full of joy. She had never felt this way before in her life!

\* \* \*

By the time Gloria returned to Pax three days later, late in the afternoon, there was already a letter from Virgil waiting for her. She read it eagerly, clasped it to her chest, and sighed longingly and happily.

Shirley watched Gloria, still standing on the quarterdeck, holding the prized letter—so it seemed to Shirley.

Ginny emerged from the lounge. "Hey, Glore! You're back! How'd it go?"

"Honey, you can nevuh imagine how guh-reat it was! I saw him again. It was so nahce."

"Let's go to evening chow together, before chow hall closes, and you can fill me in on the details. Okay?"

"Shu-uh, Gin. Jus' let me drop off mah flaght bag and wash up. Ah'll be right back down, and we'll leave then."

"Right!"

While Ginny waited, Shirley said, "Well, well, well. Look who's coming up the ladder from outside. Elizabeth Holmes, yet. And with Ensign Littleton. He's carrying her flight bag for her. They must've been on the same flight."

"See you later, Elizabeth," Ens. Littleton said, as he handed over her green flight bag. I'll be back in an hour. That enough time for you to get ready to go out for dinner?"

"Oh, yes, Mr. Littleton. Plenty of time. See you then."

Ens. Littleton departed. The phone rang and Shirley answered it, identifying herself. The caller said, "This is Lieutenant Mason. Did Elizabeth Holmes come in from her flight yet?"

"Yessir!" Holding the phone against her shoulder, she called to Elizabeth to return for the phone call."

Elizabeth took the phone from Shirley. "Hello?"

"Elizabeth! This is George Mason. Have a good flight? And how about dinner tonight?"

"Oh, Lieutenant Mason, I had a wonderful flight. However, I have an engagement for dinner. But thank you, anyway."

"Well, then," he pursued. "How about we go to the Officers Club for a drink afterward? I know that you can go there if you're accompanied by an officer. Just call me when you get back from dinner."

"Sure. We could do that. Going to your club would be so nice. I'm really looking forward to seeing you again, Lieutenant."

The air was heavy with expectation. They ended the call and Elizabeth blithely went to the second deck to get ready for her first date of the evening. She never seemed to tire. And it was a good thing, for the men who chased after her never got tired of the chase.

Meanwhile, Gloria returned to the quarterdeck, and she and Ginny departed for the chow hall. It was a leisurely walk up the hill. Gloria seemed preoccupied, and Ginny noticed it.

After they sat down with their trays of the light meal (Navy noon meals were the heaviest; dinner meals were much lighter.) Ginny opened the conversation with an inquiry about Sgt. Blake.

Gloria's face lit up like a marquee. She liked nothing better than talking about Virgil. "Oh, Ginny, he's fine. Just fine. In fact, Ah'd say much bettah than fine!"

"My goodness. What does all that mean? You getting serious about him?" asked Ginny.

"You can say that—and a lot mo-uh. Well, Ah don't mean what that *sounds* like. What Ah mean, Gin, is that Ah'm really, really fond of the Sahgeant . . ." She thought about that, then continued. "He means mo-uh and mo-uh to me with ev-rah passin' day. It feels good, Gin. Real good."

"You seem happy about that."

"You got that raght, Hon!"

\* \* \*

Lt. Albertson raced up the front steps of the WAVES barracks. Once on the quarterdeck, he approached Shirley.

"Don't tell me," Shirley said to him. "You're looking for Elizabeth Holmes. Right?"

"Right on! Is she here? Is she really here?" His eagerness was contagious.

"She was, Lieutenant. But, dear me, you've just missed her again. She went out to dinner."

"Maybe I can catch her after dinner?"

"Afraid not, Sir. She has another date as soon as she gets back from dinner. Looks as though you've missed her entirely."

"Damn! . . . Sorry about that." He blushed. "I can't make even the smallest connection with her!"

"Better luck next time?" Shirley said, half-heartedly. She was half enjoying Elizabeth's manipulating the various and sundry men in her life and half impatient with Elizabeth and her games.

"In my dreams!" He stormed out of the barracks, plainly in a snit. Immediately, he returned to the quarterdeck.

"Shirley, isn't it?" he asked her.

"Yes, Sir."

"Well, I got *that* right!"

"Yessir." *And I'm glad to hear that much from you, my poor Lieutenant Albertson. I don't think I'll ever get your name wrong.* She wondered soberly how that thought ever found its way into her consciousness.

"Thanks, Shirley."

"For what, Sir?"

"For being here and for listening to my pitiful whining."

"Not a problem, Sir. I can add it to my job description."

They laughed together.

Shirley had a thought. "Sir, would you like to have a cup of coffee? We have a coffee mess just in the next room."

"Hey! I'd like that. Should hit the spot."

She left her desk/counter long enough to slip into the next room, pour the two coffees, and return.

She had assumed that the Lieutenant took his coffee black. She assumed correctly. He took a guarded sip, knowing it would be scalding hot—and probably strong and bitter as bile. He wasn't wrong.

"Mm, mm. Now this is a cup of REAL coffee!"

"And spoken like a real Navy man!" she exclaimed.

"I tell you, Shirley, I'm beginning to feel like a real Navy man. More refresher classes to attend, more check-out flights to fly. Seems to be no end to learning new stuff and practicing it over and over, not to mention practicing the old stuff."

"Well, Sir, that's all part of the program. Learn and practice."

"How did you get so wise?"

"Sir?"

"Never mind." They chatted some more, briefly, and finished the coffees.

"Well, I gotta go. Thanks for the java."

"You're welcome, Lieutenant. Maybe we can do the coffee again, next time you come here."

He smiled at her. The barracks door closed behind him. He caught himself up short and thought, *Next time I come here? That means I'd be asking about Elizabeth. I just realized, I hadn't thought about her for the last ten minutes! I must be slipping. What the heck is that all about?*

# Chapter Three

Helen Enasevich was born in 1921 in Genesee, Michigan. After high school graduation, she worked for three years on the inspection line at the AC Spark Plug factory. At age 21, in 1942, she enlisted in the Navy. After boot camp, she was sent to the Aviation Machinist's Mate School at NAS Norman, Oklahoma. Following that, she reported to NAS Pensacola, Florida, for duty as an aviation machinist's mate, on the flight line.

Helen was a short, ash blonde Midwestern young woman. She looked fantastic in her Navy uniform, her soft brown eyes belying her personality. She was strong and indefatigable.

In 1946 Helen transferred to VR-3 at Pax River to attend flight attendant school. The two checkout flights followed.

After two years of flight-attendant experience, Helen, flying with one of the dwindling number of male flight attendants, was on a flight to deecee, Westover, and the Azores. It proceeded without incident. She could not say the same for the flight to Port Lyautey, Morocco.

Thirty minutes after passing the PNR (point of no return), out of the Azores, the aircraft lost engines No. 3 and No. 4. Immediately following that, radio and navigation equipment began to operate erratically. Later, the equipment failed completely.

The crew in the cockpit were helpless to find their way except by dead reckoning. The plane crashed in the desert.

* * *

Helen awakened, or came to—she wasn't sure which—at dusk. She was disoriented. A vast sea of sand lay before her. She was still in her seat, seatbelt fastened. She undid the seatbelt and stood up carefully. Her seat, in the tail section of the plane, was still attached to the deck, but there was no deck in front of her.

She walked around the detached tail section and spotted the rest of the aircraft *behind* the tail section. This made her feel more disoriented. Somehow, she guessed, the tail section had broken off from the aircraft upon impact and spun 180 degrees.

Quickly, she ran to the torn fuselage, hoping to find someone else alive. But she was the only survivor. Everyone was dead. She was devastated. Still shaken, she offered up a prayer for all who were lost. Then, singling out her flight-attendant partner, Tom Garret, she said, *Dear Lord, Tom was a fine young man—respectful and polite, hard-working, often doing more than his share. Keep Tom safe, Lord, in your heavenly realm. I pray in His Name. Amen.*

Then she knew she had to think about extending her survival of the crash. She took inventory of the food and beverages that were left: a couple of box lunches, some coffee, juice, and water. It took several trips to carry all that and three blankets and some pillows back to the tail section. She would use that as her shelter, for a portion of an extended part of the overhead of the tail section was intact.

Making a "bed" took some arranging and re-arranging. Sleeping on a blanket on the sand would have to do. The remaining blankets would keep her warm during the cold desert night.

She told herself to get some sleep and think further, in the morning, about her survival. Shock and exhaustion put her to sleep.

\* \* \*

On the third day after the crash, Helen, after much praying and hoping against hope, awoke and parceled out to herself the last remnants of food: a piece of bread with half a slice of cheese, and a swallow of juice. She knew she would die, here in the desert, but she tried not to think about it. She had made her peace with God, early on, after the crash.

She sat in her aircraft seat, looking out onto the sandy scene. She blinked her eyes. Blinked again. *I must be hallucinating. No, it's a mirage. I'm seeing a small band of horses coming over the ridge. Yes, it is a mirage.*

Helen kept staring at the mirage, knowing in her head and her heart that this is to be expected, after a few days of staring at the sand, sun boiling down onto her tail-section shelter. She couldn't take her eyes off the mirage, for it seemed to get larger and closer.

They pulled up about 20 yards ahead of her. Three of the horsemen alighted and walked toward her while the others approached the main body of the crashed aircraft. One of the three coming toward her spoke to her in a language unfamiliar to her.

*Wait! Mirages don't speak. Do they? Are they real? My mirage has turned into a miracle!* She passed out and slumped into a heap on the sand.

When she opened her eyes, one of the horsemen had propped her up against his body. She said, "Am I dreaming?" No response. "Does anyone here speak English?"

The horseman propping her up said with a deep, gruff voice, heavy with some kind of accent, "I speak the English. A little."

*Glory be!* she thought. She sat up. She continued to ask questions. The Arab horseman answered with grunts and nods and many gestures.

She picked up her empty paper cup and said, "Water?" Then she put the cup to her mouth and tilted her head back. The horseman stood up, went to his horse, and brought back a goatskin water bag and poured some water into her cup.

"Oh, thanks," she breathed. He simply looked at her and began again with the strange language, sometimes shouting at the others.

What she could make out was that after they looted the valuables from the corpses and luggage and anything that could be taken from the aircraft, and after they confiscated her purse, they urged her onto one of the horses, behind the English-speaking nomad. They galloped off across the sand, and she assumed there was a camp to which they would take her. What was to become of her then, she hadn't the slightest idea.

She was now in fear of things as bad, or worse, than dying. She was scared witless and was barely able to hang on to the Arab to keep from falling off the horse.

The longer they rode, the greater her apprehension grew. She didn't know how long they rode. Forever, it seemed to her. She was almost beside herself when the band of horsemen came to a stop at an oasis. This was their camp. They alighted and attended to their mounts. She was directed, she assumed, to dismount and follow the English-speaking nomad.

He led her to a tent and entered first, dragging her behind him. She was paralyzed with fear by now.

She was aware of many voices, all seeming to speak at once, and they were definitely female voices. When her eyes became accustomed to the darkness of the tent, she saw the women. They were all gaping at her, babbling to each other, touching her shirt, her tie (hanging from the left-side button, under the collar) her slacks, her shoes, her hair, her face. It made her feel crawly. She wished they'd stop pawing her like that!

In time, she got the idea that they wanted her to sit down on a rug, and the women left. Helen was so thirsty, she could spit cotton, as the saying went.

She looked around and saw there were three pottery urns in the tent. They all contained liquids. She sniffed each one and decided she'd best not try any of them. Could be poison!....to her, not knowing their customs and foods and drink. She began to worry even more. What was to become of her?

The ride had been arduous for her, and she felt sleep creeping upon her. She lay down on the rug and soon was oblivious to all that had happened to her.

The tent was even darker as someone touched her on the shoulder and woke her up. She tried to ascertain which was in the tent with her—male or female? The person spoke, and Helen heaved a sigh of relief. The voice was female.

The woman had brought Helen's purse and gave it to her. She also had brought a plate of dried fruit and what may have been some kind of dried meat. Helen didn't care what it was. She was starved. What to do, though, about water?

It was as though the woman knew what she was thinking. She produced a gourd and presented it to Helen. She gave it a tiny taste. *Glory be! It's water! Pure, sweet, heavenly water!* She was so grateful, she said to the woman, "Honey, you've saved my life—with the food and the water! Thank you from the bottom of my heart." Water was later provided for minimum bathing. The woman uttered some sounds to Helen and then left. Helen was left alone for the rest of the night. She did, however, need to use a toilet facility. She stepped to the tent flap, pulled it back, and went outside. Immediately, an improbably strong hand stopped her in her tracks.

In that strange language, he called out, not to her, but to someone in the camp. That someone came to them. It was the English-speaking Arab. He said to her, "What want?"

She said simply, "Toilet."

He took her by the arm and roughly led her to a nearby lean-to. It was a desert-model shelter, to be used for a toilet. She used it as best as she could. The Arab waited for her.

*Evidently he's guarding me so that I won't escape. Why would anyone want to escape from food and shelter? Why is he guarding me, for heaven's sake? What's going on?*

After Helen went through her purse, looking for comb, nail file, and various other items, she realized her wallet was not in the purse. *Well, that figures! There goes my money and my ID. What next?*

Four days later, she got an inkling of what was going on, and why she was being held as a virtual prisoner. That was the day Abdul Goshen arrived. He was the chief of his tribe, Emir of his emirate, son of a wealthy former emir, now deceased. One of the horsemen in the discovery and rescue party had been dispatched to the nearest emirate outpost to report on what had been found.

Goshen introduced himself on that day of his arrival, after he entered her tent. He spoke to her in impeccable English. He had been educated in both America and England. She was stunned. She was impressed by his western manners and uncommonly swarthy good looks. He was not tall but was muscular. He was dressed in jodhpurs and leather boots, a white silk shirt and white silk headpiece.

*Whoa, girl. Get a grip on yourself! This completely foreign and maybe hostile chunk of manhood is beautiful! Too beautiful for words! He even reminds me of Valentino's The Sheik. Get back to earth, Helen, and now!*

She couldn't get enough of him, staring at him as they talked. They ate dinner together in her tent.

He addressed her as Miss Enasevich. She asked, "How do you know my name?"

"I took the liberty, of course, to examine the papers in your wallet."

"What nerve!"

He was not surprised at her outburst. He said, "Here is your wallet, almost intact. Please examine it. Removing it from your person was a necessary precaution, you see?"

"No, I don't see! What is to become of me?" She looked inside the wallet. What little money had been in it was now gone, but her ID was okay.

"That is yet to be determined, Miss Enasevich."

"What exactly does that mean?"

"I radioed to the nearest naval base, in Morocco. My lieutenant, Mulsade, had sent me a description of your aircraft, complete with numbers. I informed your government that your plane has been found and that all passengers and crew are dead but one and that she is in my custody.

"Your custody! Your custody?" She was incredulous.

"It is a hard four-day ride back to the outpost. My messenger has already begun the journey. Then, after your government communicates instructions to the outpost, it is another four-day ride for my messenger to come back to camp with those instructions. We must wait for a reply from your government to see what disposition is to be made of your . . . situation."

"And just what *is* my situation?"

"See for yourself, Miss Enasevich. You have been rescued from the wreckage of your aircraft. You have been brought to this camp. You've been housed and fed. You must be returned to your people, somehow, some time. No?"

"Not no. Yes!"

*What am I saying? This man is too gorgeous for me to want to leave! What am I thinking? I must be out of my head! I must get my feet back on the ground! Must, must, must! Can't I think of anything other than must?*

Abdul sighed. *I thought I knew American and English women. But this one has me puzzled. She hasn't been violated by my men, I know, upon the word of my lieutenant, Mulsade. She is not outraged, precisely, but she is so . . . the word escapes me at the moment . . . so captivating. That's it—captivating!*

He caught himself staring at her. He got up from the rug they shared for that evening meal and left the tent.

"Well," she said after him, "and a good night to you, too!"

The next morning, three of the women entered her tent. They brought a tub and urns of wash water. They bathed her thoroughly, then washed her clothes. Helen thought, *Thank goodness! I needed that!* Then they dressed her in some of the finest garbs they had in the camp: lengths of multi-layered chiffon to form a long skirt (with generous slits in the sides), embroidered silk bra (or whatever it would be called in Arabic, she thought), more chiffon for the head, and velvet slippers. An arm bracelet and a heavy necklace completed her outfit.

Helen needed a mirror. She could only imagine what she looked like in this garb, with her ash blonde hair, brown eyes, fair skin, short stature. Everything seemed to fit all right. The yards of chiffon could be rolled up and tucked here and there to fit any figure, so it seemed to her. Even without a mirror, she was pleased with the transformation.

Another garment had been made available to her—the kaftan, many of them. Later, it was to become her choice of outerwear.

That evening, Mulsade pulled open the flap of "her" tent, took her by the arm, and said, "You. Come."

He took her to another tent. Upon entering, her eyes took a few moments to grow accustomed to the darkened tent. She could not believe what she saw. Rugs everywhere, velvet and silk cushions all over the place; low, intricately carved table legs with brass trays were in evidence in several locations; and silk draperies hung from the overhead to create "rooms."

She was aghast and agog. This must be Goshen's tent, was her first thought. But he was not in evidence. She stood in the lavishly furnished tent, waiting—for what?—and wondering.

Then, a flap at the far end of the tent was pulled back, and Abdul Goshen entered. "Good evening, Miss Enasevich. You are a vision in Arab dress."

She was flabbergasted. "Well, thank you, sir."

"Please," he said, "sit beside me here." He sat upon an array of cushions, leaving some for her to be seated on, next to him.

She sat down, saying nothing. Waiting. Food and drink were served. Toward the end of the meal, she said to him, "For desert fare, this is mighty sumptuous, sir."

"I am Emir, after all!"

"Yes, of course. How could I forget?"

"Do I detect a bit of snideness, Miss Enasevich?"

"Mmm. Maybe so. I'm a bit miffed that it's going to take such a long time to get word about my leaving here!"

"Ah, that pains me to hear you are concerned about leaving. Are not the amenities shown by me and my people meeting your needs and satisfaction? Say the word, and I shall do my best to make everything comfortable and right for you."

*Well, your highness. Actually, I am comfortable. But actually, not quite everything is right for me. How could she say that to him? She was enjoying the moment . . . .actually!*

What she said to him was, "Well, sir. Actually I am reasonably comfortable, for desert living, I'm sure. But then," she paused while she thought out how to say the next thing. "But then, although I'm anxious to go home, your hospitality is beyond reproach!"

"Ah. I am happy to hear that!"

At the end of the meal that took an hour and a half to be served and to be consumed, Abdul said to her, "Tomorrow evening, after dining, I have a surprise for you—all in the name of keeping you content during your stay with us."

She asked, "I love surprises, but can you give me a hint?"

"A hint? Let me see. I can say that it has three elements and that it is my earnest hope that you will enjoy it to the fullest!"

Upon that announcement, he arose, gave her his hand to pull her up from the cushions, and led her to her tent entrance. He kissed her hand, European style. She was abashed.

She was thrilled. She was . . . *losing it! Why do I feel as though I'm falling into a deep pit? What's happening to me?*

She slept soundly.

The next day, she wore one of the kaftans—much more comfortable than the draped chiffon clothing. But late in the afternoon, her working uniform was brought back to her by one of the women. Mulsade had accompanied the Arab woman and, pointing to Helen's stack of folded uniform, said, "You wear . . . now."

That evening, after they had completed dinner, Abdul presented her with his surprise. He led her to two saddled horses, assisted her to mount one, and then he mounted his own steed.

Following his lead, they left the camp and traveled for a good 45 minutes, at which time they arrived at a ruins.

"What's this? Ruins in the middle of the desert? The structure is made of rocks. There are no rocks nearby!"

"Very astute of you to notice that—about the construction. A long-ago-forgotten European invader built this fortress, using imported blocks of stone. In later years, the nomads rose up against him and devastated the fortress. This is what is left."

He led her to a parapet that had survived the sacking, where they could look out over the desert. It was a full-moon night. It was breathtaking. Helen didn't know what to make of it.

She asked, "So, this is the surprise? Along with the long ride on horses?"

"Yes. The third element is yet to come."

"Well, I can hardly wait. So far, it's been wonderful!"

"In that case," he said, "you are ready for the third part." He bent down slightly. He put his arms around her, gently, at first, then more aggressively. And he kissed her so passionately that she nearly lost her breath.

What really surprised her was not his kissing her, but how she reacted—by kissing him back as passionately as he had given.

They remained clasping each other, her head against him now. She was breathing erratically, almost gasping. He kissed her once more until she thought she would faint.

She pulled away and said, "Whoa, your Emirence, or whatever I should call you. Take it easy!"

"You did not like the third surprise?" he asked, puzzled once more. All the American women he had kissed before were out of their minds with joy to be kissed like that.

"Oh, don't get me wrong, sir. I *did* like the surprise. And a real, live surprise it was." Another pause. "Kiss me again, Sir Goshen, or whatever I should call you."

He obliged. She withdrew once more with a deep sigh.

"You may as well address me by my first name, 'Abdul,'" he said. "All the American and English women I knew did so."

"All? Does that mean many women? I'm curious, of course."

"Yes, it does mean many women. I hope that satisfies...... your curiosity?"

*Not in a million years, my dear Abdul. Not in a million years. I want to know everything about you!*

Upon their return to the camp, they alighted from their horses, and he walked her back to her tent. The guard was nowhere to be seen. He had been dismissed from his duty. Abdul took her in his arms and kissed her once more. He said, "Good night, sweet one."

"Good night, dear Prince of princes."

\* \* \*

At last word came from that other world, and plans were made to deliver Helen Enasevich, sole survivor of the desert crash, to Port Lyautey, Morocco. Then she would board one of her squadron's aircraft on a regularly scheduled flight, and would be returned to Patuxent River—by way of Washington, D.C., for de-briefing. She had been held by Arab nomads of an emirate with which the U.S. had questionable diplomatic relations.

When Abdul told her that the arrangements had been finalized, she was both elated and disappointed. This had been a heaven-on-earth experience for her, and she didn't quite want to end it. Neither did she want to give up her returning to the States. She was in a mish-mash quandary of thoughts and desires.

The day after Abdul told her about the arrangements, they began the trek: first by horse to the nearest desert town; then by Rolls Royce to Port Lyautey.

She wore borrowed jodhpurs and shirts from Abdul for the four-day ride by horses. The group was small, but large enough to supply the needs of Abdul, Helen, and a few more tribal members. And that would be for the duration of the first leg of the trip.

It was a six-day journey, altogether. Abdul was quiet, during the first day of the horse ride. Helen was paralyzed with doubt and her turmoil of mixed feelings.

At the end of the first day, in sparsely furnished tents, Abdul asked her to join him at the campfire. He took her hand and said, "Helen, my darling, I want you to be my wife."

Calling her Helen surprised her. Asking her to marry him was a monumental blow! She went on to ask, "And how many wives do you have already?" knowing that Arab countries often allowed multiple wives.

"Only three. You would be the fourth. And you would be the favorite, I swear to you!"

"Abdul, Abdul. As much as I'm flattered by your proposal, I cannot, in all good conscience become a fourth wife to an Arab. I just can't. I want you to understand. And surely you will understand. You've known American women before. You know their hangups about being number one in a man's life, the *only* one."

"Of course, I know that, Helen. But this is different. I would put away my other wives, supporting them, of course, but I would live only with you."

"Sorry, Abdul. I couldn't, and I won't. Sorry. Truly I am, Abdul. I have come to care for you a lot."

He said, "You Americans are so much in love with the word 'love.' Can I hear you say that you love me? I feel with all my being that you do."

"Oh, yes, Abdul. Besides caring for you, I do love you—so much it breaks my heart."

He took a deep breath and sighed heavily. "But not enough to marry me."

She replied. "If you were a Christian, Arab, or anything else, and believing in monogamy, I would marry you in an instant."

He sighed again. "I am so sorry, too, Helen, that you are refusing my offer. I would give you my entire world, you know. I am so taken with you!"

"Sweet, sweet Emir Abdul. I do love you so much."

He persisted. "Darling, you must go back to America, of course. Then, after your de-briefing, you could surely get leave to visit your family in Michigan. You could bring them here to the desert, all of you as my very special guests. After we were married, they would be free to return to their home in America. And I would take care of *all* the arrangements, all the expenses. Please, Helen, dear, won't you reconsider?"

She shook her head slowly. "I'm so sorry, Abdul. I'm so terribly sorry."

They kissed once more. And then they parted for their separate tents.

On the fourth day of travel by horses, they entered the desert town. It turned out that it contained one of his homes—palatial by any description. She wore a kaftan the rest of the day and for the first day of riding in the motor vehicle, a Rolls Royce. On the final day of the trek, she wore her uniform again, to be ready to board the plane immediately.

They arrived at their destination.

* * *

In Port Lyautey, and before Abdul handed her over to the U.S. Navy Liaison Officer, he took her to the home of a Moroccan friend. In a quiet room, he embraced her and kissed her with all the yearning and passion that had built up inside him.

Then he took an object from his pocket and placed it in her hand. It was an emerald ring, a huge stone, surrounded by pearls, rubies, and diamonds. It was the most exquisite thing she had ever seen. She was dazzled, and she was once more surprised.

She said, "Dear Abdul, I cannot accept this."

"But you must, my darling. Take it as a token of our love for each other. And if not for that, take it as a memento of your visit to the desert. And always, Helen, remember me. Do not forget me, ever. Promise."

She put the ring on the ring finger of her right hand. "Abdul, I could never forget you, even if I tried. I'll never forget you. Never stop loving you . . . in this very special way."

He picked up a dark blue, silken drawstring bag, from a nearby table and handed it to her. "This is something else I want you to have, dear Helen."

"More? What more could I take from you?"

"You needn't open it. I'll tell you what it is. The women at the oasis told me, before we left by horseback, that you favored the kaftan to wear during your stay in the desert."

"That's true. I did prefer it."

"That's what's in the silk bag—a kaftan—the first one you wore. It was no doubt the one you liked best. It is something more I want you to have and to remember me by."

"Dear Abdul. This . . . all this is too much!"

"I cannot do for you, nor can I give you enough, Helen. I am sincere about that. Take it, and the ring, and go in peace."

"Thank you, Abdul. Thank you so much."

One final kiss between them, and they left the room. They went through the main door to the outside. She got into the Navy car, the Navy Liaison Officer following her. The engine started. and the car pulled away. She looked back at the house they had just left and watched Abdul standing there, alone. She looked at the ring on her finger, looked back at Abdul and waved to him with that hand. He waved back.

The car turned a corner, and he was out of sight.

\* \* \*

"Helen! You're back! We didn't know when to expect you!" Shirley came from her room down the passageway. She was still off duty, until 1600. "You had quite an adventure, didn't you?"

Helen replied, "You can say that again!"

"Well, come on. Give, girl!"

Ginny, Gloria, and Jean entered the quarterdeck, on their way to noon chow. They greeted Helen as enthusiastically as Shirley had.

They all went to chow together, walking up the curved street to the chow hall. They begged Helen to tell them of her long absence, the crash in the desert, living in the desert, the de-briefing in deecee, and her leave in Michigan.

Helen was quiet, while they asked their questions. They noticed her reticence. As they finished going through the chow line, and seated themselves at a table, Jean said to her, "What happened, Helen? Nothing disastrous, I hope. . . other than the crash, that is."

"Oh, no. No, no. Actually, it was all quite wonderful."

"A cra-yush and all that time with a bunch of Arabs was wonduhful?" asked Gloria.

A dreamy look came into Helen's brown eyes. She did not answer right away. She thought she would keep certain parts of her desert experience to herself. *I have to tell them something. Nobody's noticed the ring yet. I'll wait for them to notice the ring before I tell what happened.* "Let's eat, for heaven's sake. I'm starved. And it's been a long time since I put my feet under a Navy chow hall table!"

"Oh, Helen," said Ginny, giggling. "You're too much!"

When they finished eating and picked up their trays and took them to the scullery room, Gloria let out a gasp. "Good grief, Helen, WHEH-UH did you get that ring?"

So, it was noticed, Helen thought. On the way back to the barracks, she unfolded the entire story. The other young women were amazed. They had no idea so much had happened to her. They were twittering about it yet, as they entered the barracks.

Elizabeth Holmes, for once, was unaccompanied by some squadron officer. She was on her way out to go on her next flight.

"Will wonders never cease!" exclaimed Jean. "Elizabeth without a date? Impossible!"

"What do you mean, 'without a date'?" asked Gloria. "Look outside. Lieutenant Cowan has just arrived in his brand-new DeSoto to give huh a lift to the terminal. Ah'll bet he's going to be the co-pilot."

"Figures!" exclaimed Ginny.

"Amen to that!" said Gloria.

By the end of the day, Helen's story had circulated throughout the barracks. Up on second deck, where the majority of VR-3 flight attendants cubicles was located, Helen, with her dazzling ring and stunning, embroidered silk kaftan, was the center of attention for the rest of the evening, until "lights out" at 2200.

At 2300 Shirley looked up from her desk/counter to see Lt. Albertson come in. *Man alive, what's he doing here at this hour? Elizabeth's been long gone on her flight. Doesn't he know that by now?*

"Good evening, Lieutenant. Didn't you know that Elizabeth left earlier today on a flight?"

He walked up to her and said, "Yes, indeed I did know that. I just came around—out of habit, I guess—to say 'hi' and to tell you I've been thinking about what you suggested some time ago: did I ever think about dating someone else?"

"And?"

"And . . . I think it's a good idea. But you know, I still would like to get to know Elizabeth. I know her only by reputation. All the fellas she's dated talk about her incessantly. Makes me want to get to know her all the more."

He looked at Shirley and said, "Dumb, huh?"

"Well, Lieutenant, I wouldn't be so hard on myself, if I were you."

"Yes, it is dumb. I'm dumb to want what I can't get."

*Oh, yes, my dear James Albertson. Why on earth don't you look around? Open your eyes! Someone could be waiting for you—wanting you, and you'd never know it. Get a grip, Lieutenant! Indeed, get a grip yourself, Shirley.*

She shook her head to rid herself of some dangerous thoughts. Jim Albertson asked her, "You all right, Shirley?"

"Oh, yeah. I'm okay."

"Is this shift hard on you?"

"Naw, Lieutenant. I thrive on it. Or, so I keep telling myself."

"I thought so. You need a change of scenery. You get off at midnight, don't you?"

"Oh, yes, every time this month."

"What say I come back then, pick you up, and we'll go to the Civilian Cafeteria for a cup of coffee? Maybe we can come up with some ideas about this search for someone else. Is that how you put it?"

"More or less." She considered his invitation, but not for long. "I'd love to go to the Civilian Cafeteria with you tonight, Lieutenant."

\* \* \*

Five days later, Elizabeth returned from her flight. It was 1800. She entered the barracks. Shirley was on the telephone. Elizabeth went straight to her cubicle, took a shower, put on a fresh uniform, and left her flight bag on the deck, unpacked.

Elizabeth went down to the quarterdeck and greeted her date, Lt.(j.g.) Elders.

Before they departed, Elizabeth said to the MAA, "Hey, Shirley, I forgot something. I left my flight bag in the middle of the cubicle. Would you go up and move it to in front of my locker? Don't want anyone to stumble over it!"

"Sure, Elizabeth. Bye."

"Bye."

Shirley went up the ladder, found Elizabeth's cubicle and walked up to the flight bag. She looked down at it and said almost aloud, *This is an effigy of you, Elizabeth Holmes. I kick your effigy!* She kicked it vigorously, giving it a shove with her foot. It scooted crazily across the deck, slamming into the locker. *That's what I think of you and your cuteness, your blonde prettiness, your petiteness, your . . . you!*

She winced at what she had just said, mostly under her breath. She looked around, wondering if anyone had heard her. She wondered what in the world made her do that! *I can't compete with her type. I'm a tomboy in uniform, I've got carrot-red hair. And the freckles! They're scattered all across my nose! Ug-lee!* She pondered over all that on her way back to the quarterdeck. The phone was ringing.

She answered it and identified herself.

"Yeah, I thought you'd be there, Shirley. This is Jim. Jim Albertson."

Her heart skipped a beat Why? she wondered.

"Just wondering if Elizabeth arrived in the barracks yet. I know her flight came in awhile ago."

"Oh, yes, Lieutenant. She came into the barracks and already went out again."

"Moan and groan! I might have guessed! With someone else. Right? How can my timing be so lousy? Dang bust it, anyway!"

*Maybe it's destiny,* she thought. Aloud, she said, "Like I said, Lieutenant. Look around you and stop focusing on the unattainable."

"I know you're absolutely right, Shirley. I just haven't the energy to do that . . . not just yet."

"Well . . ." She waited.

"Well, Shirley, I'll see you around."

"Good-bye, Lieutenant."

"Bye for now." He almost hung up, but he said quickly, "Wait! You still on, Shirley?"

"Yes?"

"Don't you ever get any days off?"

# Chapter Four

Angela Rowen was born in Santa Barbara, California, and after high-school graduation, she worked as a waitress in a hotel dining room. By the time she was 20, it was 1944. She wanted to join the Navy, but she could get in, at the age of 20, only with one parent's consent. Her father was dead-set against her enlisting: "All those sailors, up to all kinds of mischief?" he asked. "Not *my* little girl is going in the Navy!" There was no way on earth he was going to sign the consent form.

It was left up to Angela to beg her mother to do it. After much hand-wringing and mind-wrenching, the mother realized that Angela would eventually turn 21 and then would be free to do as she liked, anyway. The mother finally signed the consent form.

Angela was sent to Yeoman's School after boot camp and was then transferred to the Bureau of Personnel in Washington, D.C. She reported to VR-3 in 1946 for flight attendant school.

Almost two years later, Angela came onto the quarterdeck, dressed in flight uniform but not carrying the green flight bag. It was the uniform of Navy blue slacks, white shirt, and black tie—no jacket. She had compelling black eyes and equally black hair. With her fair complexion, she was stunning to look at.

"So, where you going this time, Angela? Where's your bag?" And where's your jacket? The MAA on duty looked at her briefly.

"Don't need a bag to fly to Bermuda. Be back same day. And I don't need a jacket, for the Bermuda weather."

"Of course! So how long do you stay in Bermuda?"

"Only for a couple of hours, then it's back to Pax."

"Well, I hope you have a nice flight."

"Thanks."

Margaret Grover, Angela's partner for the Bermuda flight, joined her on the quarterdeck. They left the barracks together and boarded the crew bus to take them to the terminal.

The flight was flawless. However, upon arriving at Bermuda, the crew was informed that a hurricane was making its way up the U.S. east coast very rapidly now, after hovering around Florida for a few days.

Therefore, their flight back to Pax was canceled, indefinitely. Angela wondered what to do, with time on her hands, and after very little thought and no planning for this contingency, she decided to take a cab ride around the island. She told Margaret what she planned to do and asked if she'd like to do that with her. Margaret, a frugal

New Englander, calculated the cost of half the cab fare, and politely declined.

Okay," said Angela. "See you later."

The road curved toward the beach, and the cab was practically on the beach at one point. She asked the driver to stop.

She got out and said to him, "Could you come back for me in a couple of hours? I'll meet you right here. I'll be able to spot it because of that big chunk of coral here next to the road."

He told her he could and he would. He drove away.

Angela took off her shoes and socks and rolled up the legs of her uniform slacks a couple of turns. She wasn't in proper uniform for being off-duty, but for the short, one-day flight, she had no baggage to carry extra clothing.

She began walking, savoring the pungent salt air, the gentle surf, the bright turquoise color of the ocean, the marvelous blue sky—all of it.

After walking about a quarter of a mile, she sat on the sand and continued to enjoy the vista. A few minutes later, she used her purse for a pillow and lay back onto the white sand, knees flexed. She rested her overseas cap across her waist. She closed her eyes against the bright sun. She almost fell asleep, she was so much at peace with herself—with the world.

A male voice spoke to her from above. "I say, Miss, are you all right?"

She sat up and looked up, a long way up, for the man was unusually tall. "Well, of course I'm all right. I haven't been so 'all right' for a long time!"

"Indeed?"

"Yes. Indeed."

They regarded each other. He noticed her raven-black hair with eyes as black as her hair. She looked awfully young.

She noticed his sandy hair, sandy mustache, and hazel eyes. She thought he must be in his early forties, maybe mid-forties? Nice, too. Not handsome, exactly, but somewhat good-looking.

"I say, Miss . . .?"

"Rowen. Angela Rowen."

"Miss Rowen it is. You're an American, aren't you?"

"I guess the American accent gave me away. American English grates on English ears, doesn't it?"

"We're not accustomed to it. That's a certainty. But how would you know that?"

"My brother was stationed in England. He wrote us about it. It was funny. He was funny. I miss him. He was lost over the English Channel."

"I'm sorry."

"Thank you."

"I say, Miss Rowen. Would you like to take tea with me at my house? It's down the beach about a mile."

*A house on the beach?* she asked herself. *The ones I saw near Carpinteria in California were covered with 20-year-old plaster that was cracked, or they were pure tumble-down clapboard shacks.* "I'd love to do that, Mr. . . . well, now I don't know your name."

"Kurt. I realize that's a curt answer. But Kurt is sufficient."

She asked, "And is there a surname in there?"

"Beckwaithe," he replied, simply, spelling it, as well. Then he decided to elaborate. "Used to be hyphenated Beck-Waithe, but my grandfather thought it looked too 'high-toned,' was his expression, and he removed the hyphen.

"My mother tells me I'm just like my grandfather, when it came to the removal of the hyphen. She said if my grandfather hadn't done away with the hyphen, that I would have."

"How interesting, Mr. Beckwaithe."

"No, no. I insist you call me Kurt."

"Okay."

"Beckwaithe," she repeated. "I've seen 'Beckwith' in the phone book, back in California. It's similar, isn't it?"

"It might be an Americanization of Beckwaithe. What say?"

"I say it could be," she answered.

He was dressed very casually: loose cotton trousers, a nondescript polo shirt, sandals.

She smiled and silently wondered what the heck this beach house was going to look like.

He helped her to stand up. She held her hat in one hand, picked up her purse, slung the strap over her shoulder, picked up her shoes (socks tucked inside), and fell into step with him, struggling to keep up with his long stride. She was a tall young woman, but not nearly so tall as he was.

They chatted aimlessly during the walk. Suddenly, they were upon the beach house. Angela almost gasped. It was a mansion!

*What on earth was I thinking—tumble-down clapboard? Cracking plaster? Hardly!* "My goodness, Kurt, this is something straight out of a novel!"

"What is, my dear?"

"This . . . this . . . house. This setting. Fa-yun-tas-tic!"

"I was hoping you'd like it."

"Like it? I find it breathtaking!"

They entered from beach side. A male servant met them and showed them to a terrace overlooking the ocean.

Angela was so impressed, she was nearly speechless.

"Jason," Kurt said to the servant, "we have a guest for tea. Will you prepare it now, please?"

"Very good, sir." Jason was a gentleman's gentleman, appearing to be about the same age as Angela's host. Gray eyes below thinning brown hair; spare frame, nearly as tall as Beckwaithe.

"Thank you," Kurt replied.

Angela put her shoes and socks on the terrace beside her chair.

Kurt quickly said, "Oh, my dear, I'm a terrible host—get that way when I'm here at the beach, so relaxing and all. Would you like to freshen up before tea?"

"Yes, I believe I would."

"Come with me."

She picked up her socks and shoes. He led her to a bedroom/parlor with its own bathroom.

"Can you find your way back to the terrace?"

"I'm sure I can. Thanks."

He left her. She rinsed off her feet and dried them. She put on the socks. She brushed the sand off her shoes and put them on, too. She then rolled down the legs of her slacks. She washed her face and hands. She combed her hair. She checked her lipstick and repaired that. She left the room and joined Kurt on the terrace.

Jason appeared magically with tea and served it.

"Miss Rowen, or Angela, if I may?"

"Angela is fine. Please go on."

"You seem to be wearing some kind of uniform. Can you explain it all to me?"

"Yes. I'd be glad to." She told him about her position in the U.S. Navy and how it was that she was there on the beach.

"So, Kurt," she said, "what do you do for a living? Do you live here year 'round?"

"Oh, my, no. This is strictly a getaway place. Back home, one might say I'm a farmer."

"Farmer? A very prosperous farmer, is my guess." She thought better of having said that. Too intrusive. "I mean. Well, what did I mean?"

"You meant exactly what you said—a very prosperous farmer. And that's true. I have fruit trees and vegetable gardens and extensive barley fields. England uses lots of barley, you know."

"For whiskey?"

"Precisely."

Angela looked around her at the obviously expensive terrace furnishings. "Your place is so beautiful. I will hate to leave it. And as soon as I finish tea, I must go back to near where you found me and meet my cabbie. I'll need to get back to the base."

"Nonsense, my dear. Tell me where you're to meet the cab, and I'll send my chauffeur to find the driver and give him the message that you have other plans."

"And let me give you some cash to give to the driver."

"My goodness, no, Angela! We'll take care of that."

He called out, "Huntley! Are you there?"

An older gentleman, balding but sturdy enough, appeared on the terrace.

"Huntley, old chap, would you be so kind as to drive back to where Miss Rowen was when she got out of her cab, and meet her driver, and give him his fare? Miss Rowen will tell you where the meeting place is."

She told Huntley the location. He bowed slightly toward her, then to Kurt, and was on his way. Angela noticed that both Huntley and Jason were also dressed informally, suitable for the balmy weather in Bermuda.

After Huntley left, Angela had another thought. "Wait!" she exclaimed. Addressing Kurt, she said, "I need to make arrangements for getting back to the base!"

"No need for that, my dear. Huntley will drive you there. Can you stay for dinner?"

* * *

At dinner, as sumptuous as the spread for tea, Angela put forth a question she wasn't sure she should ask this very fine gentleman, so sophisticated and yet down to earth—probably the farmer in him.

She asked, "Isn't Kurt a German name?"

"Indeed it is," he answered. "My mother is German. She became an English citizen in the '20s."

"Was there family conflict during the War?" Quickly, she added, "Oh, I'm sorry, Kurt. I had no business asking you that."

"No need to apologize, my dear. Of course there was conflict felt by my mother—all her blood relatives were in Germany. Mostly, she worried about them. There was, however, no question about her returning to Germany to be with them. She was completely dedicated to her husband, my father. Still is, I'm happy to say."

Then he shifted the subject back to Angela. "And what, may I ask, are your roots? America is a true melting pot, from all that I gather."

She began, "With a name like Angela, I have to be part Italian—my mother's side. My father is a real red-white-and-blue American!"

"And that means? . . ."

"That means," she said, "that his ancestry was from the entire British Isles, plus a bit of French, and a dash of Dutch."

"My, my, that is impressive," he said.

"You're teasing me, aren't you?"

"Forgive me, dear Angela. I could not resist the urge."

He said to himself, *And what other urges do I have? Hold on, Kurt, old boy. Your mother would die of mortification if I were to tell her I had an American girl friend. Girl friend! I haven't even made a pass—not that an Englishman gentleman would do that, to anyone, I think. That doesn't mean I would not like to make a pass. She's bewitching. Those black eyes bore right into my soul. Upon my soul! I'm not making any sense at all!*

Shifting the subject herself, from Urge to Dessert, an English trifle, Angela said, "This trifle is out of this world and into the next!"

"You know about trifle?"

"Oh, yes, my English grandmother used to make it—taught my Italian mother how to make it. I love it!"

He smiled.

She smiled.

Her right hand was resting on the table. He reached out and put his hand over hers. She did not try to take away her hand. He noticed. After a few moments, he released her hand.

"And what is your father's occupation?" Kurt asked.

"He has a machine shop, doing a jillion kinds of tooling and repairing. He gets a small government contract every now and then. Nothing important. Keeps him in business, though."

She felt foolish, talking about her parents' mediocre means. To change the subject again, she asked, "So, Kurt, did you serve in the military during the War?"

"Quite so!" he replied.

"RAF?"

"Oh, my, no. Nothing that glamorous. I spent almost the entire time in Burma."

"I can't imagine doing what." It was a probing statement.

He didn't respond right away. She felt uncomfortable. He finally said, "I'm not at liberty to discuss that, my dear. So sorry."

"No, I'm sorry for being so nosey."

"It's quite all right, my dear." He stood up from the table. "Come. Let's return to the terrace. The sea breeze is cooler than what we get indoors."

He led the way, and they stood at the far edge of the terrace, listening to the surf. She looked skyward to see the vast array of stars.

Kurt took advantage of that. He kissed her soundly.

She responded, then suddenly drew back. "Wait a minute," she said. "You shouldn't have done that. *I* shouldn't have done that!"

"And why not, my dear?"

Well. Although you haven't said anything about a wife, and none is evident on the premises, surely you *do* have a wife. And that being the case, I would not want to be a part of your betrayal. . ." She trailed off.

He wanted to kiss her again, she was so beguiling. Instead, he said, "I assure you, dear Angela, there is no wife. Never has been."

"You mean you're a bachelor?" She was incredulous. He was, after all, in his early forties, or more! With obvious wealth—and unmarried? Unbelievable.

"A bachelor it is, much to the distress of my dear mother. She has been playing cupid for me for twenty years! Unsuccessfully, I might add."

"Too particular? Too fussy about what a wife should look like and speak like? Twenty years of looking must be exceedingly wearing!"

"Indeed it is, when I must endure all my mother's matchmaking ploys." He took both her hands. She leaned into him. They kissed again.

"Too fussy and too particular," she murmured.

"I'm afraid so, my dear. But I could be lucky and find just the right mate, eventually."

"If you're not too fussy and too . . ."

"Enough, my dear. Enough. I plead guilty to all that."

She sighed a big sigh and said, "I really must get back to the base. The flight should be cleared by tomorrow."

Then he sighed. "Of course. Huntley!"

Angela thanked her host profusely for an absolutely marvelous afternoon and evening—the best in her life, she declared. She was overtaken with awe at all the luxury she had been exposed to today.

Kurt brought her close to him again. "I want to make it a memorable day, as well as marvelous, Angela dear." He gave her a final kiss. They clung to each other for long moments. She savored it.

All of it.

Huntley appeared on the terrace. He cleared his throat. "Ready, Mum?" he asked.

She thought, *As ready as I can be, I guess. God, I hate to leave this place, this Garden of Eden. I especially hate to leave Kurt. No wife, eh? Oh, well. Forget it! C'est la vie.*

As she approached the small vehicle and Huntley opened the back door, she noticed a crest on the side of the front door. After a final goodbye between Angela and Kurt, Huntley started the car and drove down the lane, toward the road.

Angela asked Huntley, "Sir," she said, "what is that crest on the side of the front door?"

"You don't know, Mum?"

"I haven't a clue!"

"Didn't he tell you who he is?"

"Well, he said his name is Kurt Beckwaithe, and he said he was a farmer."

Huntley briefly lost his dignified demeanor and smiled grandly, almost laughed. "A farmer, you say? Well, Mum, that is true. He is also the Duke of Branbury, Dorset County."

"A Duke? Are you kidding me, Huntley?" She was dismayed to think she had spoken to him, a bit of royalty, so sassily from time to time.

"I do not kid anyone, Mum. I'm most serious. It is the truth I speak."

"Well, I'll be!"

\* \* \*

When Angela returned to Pax River, she was assigned to another flight two days later. This one took her to Iceland. Upon her return, Gloria, Ginny, Jean, and Helen were on the quarterdeck. "Hey, how'd it go, Angie?" asked Ginny.

"Okay. I guess."

"Engine trouble? Bad weather? Touchy passengers?" It was Helen's turn to make inquiry.

"No," Angela answered. "I'm still thinking about that little Bermuda flight that Margaret and I had. You know, the one that got delayed because of hurricane winds that came through here?"

Gloria jumped in with, "Yeah, yeah, we know, and we remembuh. We also got stuck *he-ah* for awhile. So what about Buh-myuda?"

"It's too incredible to believe!" said Angela.

"Try me," said Helen. "Tell the tale!" She was piqued with curiosity, speaking of tall tales one wouldn't believe. She had shared her own unbelievable story to these friends, her shipmates.

Shirley called out, "Angie, you got a letter while you were gone."

"From my folks?"

"Don't think so. It's foreign-looking, odd size, odd stamps. I think it might be from England." Angela's breath became shallow. Trembling a little, she reached for the letter. There was a crest on the back of the envelope, and she recognized it. She opened the envelope.

"Well?" asked Helen. "Who's it from?"

Angela said, "Let me just . . . go into the lounge and read it privately. I'm not sure what it's going to say."

They let her go, consumed with curiosity. They decided to sit on the couch and in the chairs on the quarterdeck and wait for her to come out and tell the news—about the Bermuda trip, about the letter.

They discussed it among themselves. Angela hadn't been to England lately, had she? They didn't think so. Then what's the mysterious letter from England all about?

They talked on and on about the possibilities.

Ginny and Gloria had a side conversation between themselves. Ginny asked her, "Heard from Sgt. Blake lately?"

"Oh, yes, Gin. Ah get two or three lettuhs a week."

"Whoa, girl. That's heavy correspondence going on."

"Ah know," said Gloria. "Ah really like the guy. He's so attentive when Ah see him in Germany—Bad Soden, Frankfurt, Wiesbaden. And he's equally attentive with all the lettuhs."

"So," Ginny said, "you just going to have a long-distance romance, and that's it?"

"We-ah waitin' for his duty to be up in Wiesbaden, and he's put in for duty in deecee. He may even wind up as a recruituh the-ah!"

"Hey, that'd be great, wouldn't it?"

"Oh, bettuh than great, Gin. It'd be . . ." She searched for a word . . . "glorious!"

* * *

In the lounge, Angela, hands shaking, opened the letter and read:

"My dearest Angela,

"I've started this letter a dozen times, more or less, wondering how I can say to you on paper all the things I wanted to say to you when I saw you at my home in Bermuda.

"I'm currently visiting my parents in their London apartment, where they stay most of the time, making short and infrequent visits to the 'farm' in Dorset County.

"Huntley related to me the conversation you had with him on the way to your base. Bless him! And curse him! I had hoped to keep my real identity from you—for awhile, at least.

"So why would I want to do that? As soon as you might learn who I really am, I was sure you would 'freeze,' and I would be deprived of your wonderful presence. You must know, Angela, that I was quite smitten with you as a result of that nearly half-day at the beach house. "And that brings me to the things I wanted to say to you but couldn't because of my long-standing training in propriety, and because of the infernal rules of conduct imposed upon me all my life.

"What I want to say to you is that were it not for my position in English life, I would have begged you to marry me. Yes, even after so little time we were together that day. It was enough to give me a keen insight into what sort of woman you are. It was enough to make me yearn to be with you forever—to have you in my arms once more, even now, as I write this to you.

"Further, this is a cruel thing to say to you, Angela, and I beg you to grant me a thousand pardons for it. The fact of the matter is that I <u>cannot</u> ask you to marry me. I must look for a woman who has a title.

"My mother has combed all of England and the rest of Europe in her dogged search. She wonders why I don't make a choice. I've told her over and over why, and she simply does not accept my reasons for not making a choice. The reasons are: Of all the women in the nobility that she has introduced to me, none has excited me; none has challenged me; and nearly all of them have been simpering, cloying idiots. Some others have been outright conniving and manipulative—two dangerous traits!

"Upon my return here in London, I knew that I had to confront my mother to tell her that I had met the perfect mate for me and that unfortunately, it was someone I knew she would not accept. That confrontation is yet to take place.

"You may point out to me, and rightfully so, that our own Prince Edward married an untitled woman (I use that term as opposed to 'commoner,' for it seems so . . . so common). He even gave up the throne to marry her.

"Would that I had such courage! Alas, it is not in me. Keeping the peace in my family (with my mother, specifically) is paramount in my life at this time.

"Dear, sweet Angela. I miss you so much. I dare not try to arrange a meeting with you, and I could do so, with very little difficulty. As it turns out, relations between Mother England and the upstart

America are largely very excellent. A meeting with you could be accomplished!

"Please, Angela, forgive me for not having the backbone to stand up to my mother and declare my love for you as well as declare you as my choice for a life mate. That would be my greatest wish, if such wishes were permitted in our own tight little society."

"Damn society's rules!"

"With all good wishes for your own happiness, dear Angela, I enclose with this letter a small token of my passion for you. Think of me every time you wear it. Kurt"

She reached into the out-sized envelope and removed a flattened velvet pouch. She opened it and shook out the contents. It was a delicate gold chain threaded through a medallion of some sort. She looked at it carefully and soon recognized it: the Duke's crest.

\* \* \*

When Angela emerged from the lounge, she sat down amongst the others. They waited for her to speak.

"To begin with," she said, "I met someone in Bermuda. A really very sweet and nice gentleman. Turns out that he's a Duke, the Duke of Branbury, Dorset County, in England. This letter is from him. Very personal, you understand."

They all nodded.

"And," she continued, "he sent me this." She held up the chain with the crest dangling at the end.

Jean was the first to speak. "Angie, it's magnificent!"

"It's go-uhjuss . . ." breathed Gloria.

Ginny said, "Here, Angie, let me put it around your neck and fasten it for you. You can wear it under your uniform, can't you?"

"Of course. I'll always wear it, even in the shower!"

"But just what is the significance of such a gift, Angie?" Helen asked. "An engagement present?"

Angela thought for a moment before answering. "No, there's no engagement to announce, not now and not ever. But if there were an engagement, I think this gift might have been for it."

"Girl, you-ah talkin' in circles. Explain!" Gloria demanded.

"I can't do that. It's too complicated to explain. Sorry." Angela really meant it.

They all sat in an uneasy silence.

"Well, well," Jean said. "Here comes Ensign Brickel. Wonder what he's doing here?"

Ginny said, "Three guesses!"

They all laughed together. They listened to Ens. Brickel speak to

Shirley: "Elizabeth Holmes is expecting me. Is she ready?"

\* \* \*

Angela fingered the medallion around her neck and now resting on the outside of her uniform. The others admired it anew. Finally, she excused herself to go shower and hit the sack.

Helen and Jean decided to do the same. But Ginny and Gloria remained on the quarterdeck, talking softly.

\* \* \*

After Kurt wrote the letter to Angela and posted it, he set out with strong resolve and confronted his mother in his parents' ten-room apartment in London. He had a showdown with her. It began innocuously enough, with the usual greetings between them.

Kurt dug right in. "Mother, I want to tell you something."

She was leery of his manner and said so.

He paid no attention to that and went on. "I'm 43 years old and still unmarried. I've met a young woman with whom I am completely enamored. I am deeply in love with her, but she does not begin to measure up to your requirements for a daughter-in-law. She has no title, no family money."

"What must you be thinking, Kurt?" She was astonished and clearly apprehensive at the turn of events.

"I'm thinking that I would like very much to make her my wife."

She sucked in her breath.

"However, Mother, I shall not take that step. It flies in the face of all that's expected of me and my position. I know that. It happened, anyway, my falling in love.

"So, continue, my dear Mother, to solicit the young females of our society . . ."

"Kurt! Don't be crass! Females. Really!"

"Hear me out, Mother, please. Just be sure, I'm asking you, to present to me only the young women who have a head on their shoulders. No more tizzlebrains! Please! I beg you, Mother. And if you can't find a satisfactory candidate, titled and moneyed, and with at least half a brain, I'll look for her myself!"

He turned and left the apartment.

His mother almost fainted. But she was too much in control to let that happen. She said to herself, *what's this world coming to?*

\* \* \*

"What's the latest from Sgt. Blake?" Ginny asked.

"Ah haven't seen him for a couple of months, but we still write. Ah hope Ah get Germany next flight." Gloria spoke wistfully.

"Keep the faith, Hon. Keep the faith." Ginny stood up. "Think I'll turn in early. Good night, Gloria."

"Good night, Gin."

After Ginny departed, Gloria decided to write to Virgil again even though she had written him only two days before. She borrowed paper and a pen from Shirley. Moving into the lounge where there was a writing table and the lights were still on, she began the letter:

"Dearest Virgil,

"Ginny asked about you again tody, and that has prompted me to write you again so soon after my last letter. She has been interested in our friendship and shown a lot of support. I appreciate her so much.

"Not much else to report on, but I could tell you a little bit about the base—where the chow hall is, where the chapel is, where the library is, where the base bus station is, and so on.

"The chow hall is at the top of a hill, at the far end of the curved street that fronts both the WAVES barracks and the chow hall. The street makes a full loop back to the main street. Chief's Quarters are between the WAVES barracks and the chow hall. At certain times of the day, we eat in another chow hall, which we take a bus to get to, from work, either at the hangar or at the terminal. But the barracks isn't too far from that chow hall, either. There's a fair-sized walk on a path through some trees (pines and maples); and you have to cross the main street. Then it's a short jaunt back to the barracks again.

"The main core of the base is a long string of buildings housing the Ship's Service, the bank, and our Disbursement offices. That's where we get our monthly pay checks—handy to the bank, you see. That group of buildings is the place where all station busses stop, and you can transfer to other parts of the base, as needed. The library is in one wing—a closed-off wing—of the men's barracks, on the other side of the base.

"We have a beach on the base! It's on the Patuxent River side of the base, not the Bay. Unfortunately, at certain times during the warm-weather months, no one can swim off the beach—jelly fish! They sting, if you step on one on the beach, or if you encounter one while in the water. It's simpler just to stay out of the water.

"Now for the base bus station for commercial busses. It's a short two blocks from the WAVES barracks, and on the main drag. Makes it easy to get transportation to deecee.

"The chapel. Ah, the chapel. Not big, but smallish and friendly. No soaring roof. A stained-glass window at the front, when you approach the chapel, that embraces a cross and the Star of David superimposed on the cross. A little startling upon first glance. But symbolic of the interfaith unity found in the Naval Service.

"The structure housing the chapel is unpretentious, as it should be, in my opinion. And so handy! You walk out the back door of the barracks, on the opposite side of the entrance to the quarterdeck. A stand of trees—more pines and maples—separates the barracks from the chapel. It's a short walk on a well-trod path leading from the barracks, through the trees, and to the chapel parking lot. Then on into the chapel. You have to see it in person to experience the feeling of peace and contentment within its walls.

"Enough of the base. I want to write about something else. Remember that afternoon we finished lunch at the enlisted men's dining room in Bad Soden and took a long hike to Kronenberg Castle? I think about it a lot.

"It was four miles, the last mile uphill to the castle, and four miles back. But what we hadn't expected is that when we got to the castle and entered the great hall, an Army Corporal approached us and said that the castle is an officer's club, and it was off limits for enlisted people. We weren't allowed to enter. We couldn't even sit down to rest.

"Shoosh! We were exhausted from that last mile, uphill all the way, not to mention the previous three miles through the countryside—watching a boys' soccer game, viewing the mountains in the distance, passing a boys' hiking group in their lederhosens, getting passed up by the various and sundry GIs in their cars with their German girl friends . . .

"I would have given my right arm for a chair to sit in, even for a few moments.

"And when we got back, it was dark, but we made it just in time for evening chow.

"Incidentally, after we sat down at the dining table, I looked down toward my shoes and found that the heel of my nylon hose had a hole in it! It was a hole in the seam.

"After dinner, you walked me back to my hotel, and right there, on the darkened street (no street lights working in post-war Germany yet), you kissed me so sweetly, I nearly cried.

"Goodness sakes, Virgil! It's nearly time for lights out! How I have run on. Hope it hasn't bored you to death! Bye bye for now, dearest one. I long to see you again, soon. I pray not only for a safe flight, but for another flight to Germany—to see you once more. Much love always, Gloria."

\* \* \*

"Good evening, Petty Officer Jackson."

"Good evening, Lieutenant Albertson."

He regarded her carefully. *I never noticed before that Shirley has freckles across her nose—just like me! I like that. I like that very much. I like . . .* He said to her, finally, "You're on the four-to-mid shift again, right?"

"You got it, Lieutenant." Shirley answered.

He looked at her some more and asked, "What say I come back after your shift, and you and I go to the Civilian Cafeteria again for a cup of coffee?"

She thought that would be just super and said so.

\* \* \*

In the Civilian Cafeteria, at the beginning of a new day, on the clock, they sat facing each other with their cups of coffee between them. They talked, each one, about his or her beginnings.

Shirley was born and reared in southeast Missouri, in a small town that had a general store and a cotton gin. "Pretty humble beginnings, I'm afraid," she said ruefully.

"Nothing wrong with humble, Shirley. I was born practically in a cornfield in Iowa. Talk about humble! And corny!"

They giggled over that and went on to talk about high school. A boy friend here, a sweetheart there. All in the past. A past half-forgotten, even in their young years.

She continued, "So, I enlisted in 1942. I was 21. I'd attended two years college on athletic scholarships."

"Nice," he offered.

She grinned. "Then, I worked for the recreation department in St. Louis. I finally got patriotic and enlisted!"

"Bully for you!" he exclaimed.

Another smile. "After boot camp, I was assigned an MAA job at NAS Olathe, Kansas, in the WAVES Barracks. Then I was transferred here at Pax in late 1945, also as MAA in the WAVES Barracks. I've recently re-enlisted in the Regular Navy."

"Really!?"

"True. It's my home, my life, now."

For a moment, Jim was deeply thoughtful, and asked himself, *Why do I feel sorry?*

Shirley then asked Jim to tell about his background and his war experiences.

"Not much to tell. I finished college, worked in a bank for a year, and got a commission in the Reserves in '42.

"Then, after flight school, I flew transports most of the time. Now, since the end of the War, all the time. At first, I was only the co-pilot. Now I'm a plane commander. During the war, we carried VIPs here and there; even transported some USO celebrities—could've gotten some autographs, but you don't think about that as you're landing a plane on a make-shift runway in the jungle!

"And you, Shirl? You do anything exciting?"

"Give me a break, Lieutenant. An MAA's job is exciting? Although . . . come to think of it, there was that night at NAS Olathe, when a sailor fell through the overhead of the WAVES barracks. Now that was exciting! A little too exciting, if you ask me."

They laughed until the tears came to their eyes.

Lt. Albertson said to her, "I better get you back to your barracks. We've already put a big dent in your beauty sleep!"

"I've had too much fun to be sleepy, Lieutenant."

"Would you just quit the 'Lieutenant' stuff? I do have another name, 'Jim'. Please, Shirley, use the 'Jim.'"

After waiting for the station bus and traveling half-way around the base to get to the WAVES barracks, they alighted, and Jim escorted her to the bottom steps of the barracks. He took her left hand in his right and squeezed it tightly.

Jim said, "Sleep well, MAA."

Shirley said, "I really liked being with you, Jim." *Did I ever!* "And I thank you for the coffee and the company."

"You're entirely welcome. I liked being with you, too."

She slipped her hand from his, went quickly up the steps and into the barracks.

Jim stood at the bottom step, watching her, and thinking, *She actually has legs! Nice legs, at that! Why hadn't I noticed that before? Let me see, she had on slacks the first time we went out for coffee. But tonight, she's wearing a skirt. Why hadn't I noticed the legs before? The desk! Of course, she's always been hiding behind the desk! Damn that desk!*

He walked back to the bus stop and waited for the next station bus to come by and pick him up and take him to the BOQ (Bachelor Officers Quarters). He had a lot to think about and had plenty of time to do it while he waited. *What's going on here? Neither of us mentioned Elizabeth Holmes. Not even once! I'm no longer sure I remember what she looks like . . .*

# Chapter Five

Gloria, Angela, and Ginny sat in the lounge off the quarterdeck. They talked about their flight schedules, their varied destinations, and re-hashed experiences already shared.

Gloria sat with a package of letters from Sgt. Blake. She spoke of him fondly, "Virgil is such a de-ah. We had a nice reunion last week when Ah finally got a Germany flight from the Azores."

"Care to elaborate?" Ginny asked.

"It was so nice," she began. A long pause. "It was so nice." Another pause. "But Ah already said that, didn't Ah? We hadn't seen each other for a few months. It was almost like meeting each oth-uh again for the first time....almost."

"I can't imagine my meeting someone like that—a passenger on a flight. What are the chances it would happen to all of us?" Angela asked, wistfully.

"No one could be so lucky as I've been. He's a de-ah, de-ah man."

"Any romance in this?" Ginny inquired.

Gloria looked at her. "Oh, yes. Lots!"

"And?"

"Well, if you'ah asking about marriage....."

"And I am," Ginny confirmed.

"Not until Virgil gets his hoped-fo-ah transfuh to deecee or somewheh-uh ne-ah the-ah. We're sort of just waiting for that to happen before we get down to serious talkin' about marriage."

"Sounds wise. I wish you luck. Good luck, that is. And good luck for the Sergeant's transfer," Ginny said.

"Thanks," Gloria said. "Next time ah wraht him, Ah'll tell him you said that." Another long pause. Addressing Ginny again, she asked her, "Gin, whe-ah you goin' on yo-ah next flaght?"

"Ah, you had to ask! The scheduling chief put me on the 'Ruptured Duck' for all next week!"

Angela asked, "What? You mean the 'Hernia Special'?"

"The one and the same—the daily cargo run, in an R4D," Ginny replied. "You know, the one that goes to NAS Willow Grove, Pennsylvania, and then to Harrisburg, and then back to Pax. The plane is so heavily loaded when we come back, it got the name of 'Ruptured Duck' as well as 'The Hernia Special.' It rarely has any passengers."

"You got assigned that run for a whole week? What on earth did you do to deserve THAT?" asked Angela.

Ginny said, "Well, for starters, I messed up on my last flight.

Between Newfoundland and the Azores, overnight, I failed to check at the cockpit to see if the pilots wanted something other than coffee—soup? tea? water? a glass of milk? Whatever. The pilot wrote me up! So, the scheduling chief is punishing me with the 'Ruptured Duck' run for next week."

"That's pretty gosh-awful!" Gloria commiserated.

"You can say that again," Ginny retorted. "But, let's look on the bright side: I could have been grounded!"

"You're kidding!" exclaimed Angela.

"Oh, no. But lucky for me, the scheduling chief needed someone to do the Pennsylvania run. So I lucked out by getting that instead of being grounded."

Gloria said, thoughtfully, "You ah a true optimist, you know that?"

Ginny shrugged, then smiled.

Gloria turned to Angela and asked, "Angie, you have a flaght tomorrow, don't you?"

"Yep. Azores-bound. Don't know where we'll end up, though, as you know."

"How well Ah know!" Gloria replied.

Ginny smiled agreeably.

* * *

At eight o'clock the next morning, Angela arrived at the terminal with Beth McGrath, her flight-attendant partner for this flight, and they prepared the plane's main cabin for the short leg to Washington, D.C. Then on to Westover AFB and on to Argentia.

After leaving Argentia, Newfoundland, the two flight attendants settled in for the long haul to the Azores. As the flight went on into the night, Beth took the first rest period, two hours of sleep.

Angela was on duty by herself. Most of the passengers slept. One of the radiomen, who was off duty at the moment, came aft to get some coffee.

He said, "A cup of coffee, please? And put a head on it!"

Angela drew it from the urn. The cup of coffee had several air bubbles on the top. She handed it to him, saying, "One cup of coffee, with a head on it!"

The radioman smiled at her, appreciating her wit. He hung around and after awhile, he asked her how she liked flying.

"Like it fine. How 'bout you?"

"Best duty I ever had!"

"Well," she said, glancing at his rating badge, noting that he was a radioman, first class, and then at his name badge (William Wagner), and finally at his one hash mark. "I suppose you've had a bit of duty.

I see you're wearing at least one hash mark."

"Yeah. Been in six years, actually."

"And you're a first class?"

"Yep. I came in as 2nd class."

"Well! How the heck did you do that?"

He told her the testing process he had gone through in the Naval Reserve. "I figure to make Chief next time around. Hope so, anyway."

"Well, I hope you make it, too. Good for morale, don't you think . . . 'Bill'? Is that right?" He nodded.

He looked into her black eyes, admired them immensely, and said, "Sure is good for morale." He made a decision: he continued, "We get into the Azores early in the morning. After our rest period, how 'bout you and I meet at the chow hall, have evening chow together, and then go to the NCO (non-commissioned officers) Club? They have a live band on Saturday nights, and dancing."

She looked straight back at him. He was only medium height so that she could look into his warm hazel eyes. She said, "Is that supposed to be a date, or something?"

"I don't know about the 'or something,' but yes, it is definitely supposed to be a date!"

"Done!" she said.

Then he asked, "By the way, are you Beth or Angela? Can't tell which is which, because, on the crew's list, you're both first-class petty officers."

"I'm Angela, or Angie. Beth is asleep."

"Got it! Don't forget our date, Angie."

"Not a chance."

\* \* \*

At the beginning of the evening, in the chow hall, they ate together. The Air Force was more lenient than the Navy when it came to having military men and women eating together in the chow hall.

They talked about inane things: where they had been on their flights, duties between flights, how's the chow at Pax, how's the chow at this Air Force Base at Lagens, Azores, and what did they think of their plane commander and co-pilot for this flight?.

Later, at the NCO Club, they danced every dance, before the band's first break. Then he led her back to their table when, still holding her hand, he stopped at the edge of the dance floor.

"What?" she asked.

He said, "Let's go out on the porch for awhile."

"Okay."

When they left the club, and he let the door close behind them, he walked her around the corner of the porch. He said to her, "Angie, I want in the worst way to kiss you."

"Then, why don't you?"

\* \* \*

The next morning, the crew was ready to report for the next flight. There had been a pileup of aircraft with crews so that Angela's flight wouldn't be assigned until the next day. Beth returned to the barracks.

Angela had tarried in the billeting office, in the middle of the many barracks buildings on the base in the Azores, hoping to catch Maria, an Azorean young woman who did laundry for crew members that needed it done during unexpected waiting periods in the Azores. Angela wanted to engage Maria for doing some personal laundry.

While Angela waited, Bill appeared, to get the "skinny" on their next flight. He saw her right away and called out to her, "Hey, Angie! What's the scoop?"

She explained about the pileup of crews and that they'd be another day in the Azores before flying out.

"Well, that leaves us with just one thing to do," he said to her.

"And what might that be?"

"We can take a walk around the base, catch a bus into town, window-shop, have coffee at a little café, and wend our way back to the base for noon chow."

"My goodness! How did you dream up all that in such a short time?"

He snapped his fingers. "Just like that." He opened the door for her and said, "Come on. Time's a-wasting."

Angela's thoughts centered on Maria. *Whoops. I'm going to miss seeing Maria about my laundry. Oh, well . . . I smell adventure ahead, sort of.*

They strolled toward the edge of the base that ended in a steep cliff to the ocean below. They couldn't go all the way to the edge because a fence and a sign told them it was "off limits."

Making their way to the "front" of the base, the fence ended, and they were able to walk on an Azorean road, up the hills and down the hills. Stone fences bordered the various fields everywhere. An occasional stray dog approached to sniff their shoes. Suddenly a rain shower descended upon them.

They looked at each other and laughed, for it was going to be a long run to get to any shelter, which would be the Main Gate. Forget running, they agreed. They were already drenched when a jeep approached from behind, stopped, and gave them a ride into town. By the time they arrived there, the rain had ceased. Angela felt of her hair, that which showed beneath her hat. It was straight as a stick. "I must look like a clown!" she exclaimed.

"A very lovely clown, if I may say so."

"You may say so." She smiled in spite of her apprehension about how she must look, bedraggled, and soaked to the skin.

They alighted at the town square. They walked in and out of the shops. They encountered the café that Bill had alluded to. They went in for coffee.

"Ugh!" Angela exclaimed. "This coffee's terrible! So strong . . . and bitter to boot!"

He sniffed his coffee. "A-a-ah. Now this is like shipboard coffee!"

She said, "I know that Navy coffee is strong, and sailors are supposed to like it, but *this*, Bill., is a bit much!"

"No, no. Take another sip, Angie. You *can* get used to it. May take time, however."

"Bill," she said, after taking another sip, "*You're* a case!"

He laughed. She liked his laugh. She smiled amply. She said, "You know, Bill? I've really enjoyed myself, being with you this morning. It was a great idea to do the hike and come into town. Even if we did get rained on! Thanks a lot."

"We still got an afternoon and evening to fill up. And I have ideas for that, too."

"I'll just bet you have."

\* \* \*

After they returned to the base and changed clothes, and ate at the noon chow, they went to a matinee movie on the base. They had evening chow together in the chow hall. They went to the NCO Club again. Juke-box music didn't appeal to either one of them. They went out to the porch, just as they had the evening before. They kissed once more, just as they had the evening before.

"Angie, honey. I certainly hope we can have flights together again and even better than that, have between-flights-time together."

"Oh, Bill. You have to know, I would like nothing better than that. You're really a great guy."

"And you, Angie. You're the best!"

They kissed once more. He took her by the hand and said, "Come on. I'll walk you back to your barracks."

\* \* \*

By the time their flights to Port Lyautey, back to the Azores, and back to Pax were completed, Bill had asked her if they could see each other on a regular basis—schedules permitting. She agreed.

On the crew's bus to the WAVES barracks, back at Pax, she thought about the flight she had just completed. *Be darned if I didn't meet someone on a flight! It wasn't a passenger; it was a crew member. Never thought that'd happen to me! Bill Wagner. Bill Wagner. Don't remember seeing him around. I guess it takes the confined space of an aircraft to make people notice each other. I'm glad he noticed. I'm glad I noticed, too.*

Angela and Beth entered the quarterdeck and spoke to Shirley. "Hey, we're back!"

"So I see," said Shirley. "Where'd you go?"

"Port Lyautey," Beth explained. "I'm pooped! I'm going straight to the shower and hit the sack!" She turned on her heel and, dragging the green flight bag alongside, trudged up the ladder, pulling off her hat and leaving her short blonde hair hanging limply against her head. "Man, do I need a shower—and a shampoo," she muttered, beyond hearing range of the others.

Helen was picking up her mail at the quarterdeck and asked Angela, "Run into any sheiks while you were in Morocco?"

"Alas, Helen, no! And I don't think I nor anyone else can top, let alone match, *your* encounter!"

Helen answered, "Well, then, did you run into any more dukes on the way?"

"Will you stop it with the jokes, Helen?" Her face lit up, and she continued. "But I did run into someone."

"So, let's hear about it!" Shirley put in.

"Oh, gosh, it was absolutely splendid. I met someone on the plane, and he's a crew member from our own squadron! One of the radiomen."

"Do we know him?" asked Helen.

"I dunno. Maybe you do. If he asked you for a date during a flight, you might've met him."

"Are you kidding?" asked Helen. "Elizabeth Holmes has all the enlisted men mad at us because it looks as though officers are the only squadron men we date!"

Angela said soberly, "So it seems." After a pause, "But we know it's not true, not for all of us, anyway."

"And speaking of the Devil," Shirley interjected, "here comes Elizabeth Holmes, herself, on the arm of . . ." She squinted to see this latest escort. "Someone new, perhaps. But of course!"

Helen recognized him. "Lieutenant Simms, I think. He *is* new."

"Not to Elizabeth, it appears," said Shirley.

"New, old, in-between. Elizabeth knows them all!" That came from Angela.

Laughing all the way, Angela and Helen went together to evening chow. But before they passed through the barracks front door, on their way out, the phone began ringing.

Shirley answered, "WAVES Barracks, Master-at-Arms Jackson speaking."

It was for Angela. Shirley called her back. Angela took the phone from Shirley and said, "Hello?"

"Hiya, Angie. It's Bill. If you're not too exhausted, let me pick you up at your barracks, after you've had evening chow, and we'll walk to the gym to see the movie."

"Man, you are a fast worker!"

"That's what I like to hear. See you in a little while." He hung up.

Angela stood at the MAA desk/counter, looking at the silent telephone. *I feel like I just waltzed through a whirlwind. . .*

She hung up, and as she and Helen left the quarterdeck, the phone rang again. And again Shirley answered, "WAVES Barracks. Master-at-Arms Jackson speaking."

A familiar voice said back to her, "Hey, Shirl, what's up?"

She recognized Jim's telephone voice from so many phone calls from him by now. She answered, "Oh, just your standard slow watch in the WAVES Barracks. You just get in?"

"Yes."

"You must have been on the same flight with Angela and Beth."

"I believe so. Yeah, that's right." He hadn't really noticed who the flight attendants were, not even looking anymore for Elizabeth to be on his flight.

She said softly into the phone, "I'm so glad you're back safely."

He smiled and said, "So am I, if truth be known. Say, Shirl, is there any Rule or Regulation against your having a visitor while you're on duty?"

"Not that I know of." She waited breathlessly. *Is he really coming over just to see me? And not inquire about Elizabeth? For once?*

"Well, then," he said, "I'm going to officer's mess now, and as soon as I'm finished, I'll be right over on the first bus that comes by! And, Shirl, when's your next day off?"

\* \* \*

The next day, Bill Wagner paid a visit to the scheduling Chief...and tried to make a deal, "What would it take to get me on the same flight assignments as someone else?" Bill asked.

"No problem," said the Chief. "What's her name?"

The next month, the Chief called Bill and asked him to come to his office. "Sorry, Wagner," he said. "The party is over."

"Whaddaya mean?"

"My boss realized what I was doing with the schedules. He made me cease and desist!"

"Darn!"

# Chapter Six

Helen Enesevich was dead-tired from her last flight: delay in the Azores, delay in Iceland, and a delay at Sydney, Nova Scotia, which had been an alternate stop because of weather at Westover—and for having low fuel on board, heavy headwinds being the cause of that.

However, she was determined to go to noon chow, anyway. She knew she'd probably sleep for hours, missing evening chow altogether. In that case, she would awaken in the middle of the night, half starved!

Helen dropped off the ubiquitous green flight bag on the quarterdeck, running outside to catch a bus for the alternate chow hall. When she alighted from the bus at that chow hall, she said to herself, *Good grief! Look at that chow line, out the door, down the steps, and into the parking lot!* She made her way toward the end of the chow line when a voice called out, "Hey, Helen! Is that you, Helen?"

She looked at the young man calling to her—by her name, yet. She didn't recognize him, but smiled and asked, "And how do you know who I am? I don't believe I know you."

"Don't you remember me, Helen?" he asked. "Study Hall? Kelley High School? Genesee, Michigan?"

She looked at him more closely. He was mentioning names she was well acquainted with—her high school, her town! He was a bit on the short side, blond, brown eyes, a hopelessly engaging smile.

"Good heavens!" she exclaimed. "Of course I remember you. Rob Erwin! Couldn't place you at first because I never dreamed I'd see you again—not here, especially! So, you're in the Navy? What's your rate?" He was wearing a ground crewman's work jacket, dungarees, watch cap. His rating badge was not visible.

"Oh, I'm just an aviation machinist's mate, second class. I'm in VR-3."

"For heaven's sake, we're in the same squadron? You're four years younger than I am. And you're already in the Navy? Must've enlisted as soon as you turned 17."

"I did!" He motioned for her to take her place ahead of him in the chow line. "Come on, Helen, you can drag the line here."

"Oh, no, Rob, I wouldn't dream of doing that. I'll go on to the back of the line."

"Nah, you don't have to do that. Does she, fellas? Okay if she drag the line here?" he asked, grinning widely.

"Sure." "Sure." "Sure." "Go ahead," they said, and gave him a sly wink in the process.

So they walked up to the chow hall together. Time to chat, time to get re-acquainted. She said, "You know, Rob, before I came to VR-3 and changed my rate, I was an aviation mech, too."

"You were? No kidding!"

"That's right. No kidding."

"What was that like? For a girl...er...woman, I mean."

"It was no picnic, I tell you! I was stationed at NAS Pensacola, Florida. The men on the flight line would let me gas the aircraft, but little else. I spent most of the time in the flight-line office, shuffling papers."

"Crumby!"

Now they were inside the chow hall, and they filled their trays. At the end of the chow line counter, Rob went to the left, and Helen went to the right. In those days, sailors and WAVES were not permitted to eat together. Upon finishing their meals, they met at the front door of the chow hall.

Rob asked, "You going back to work, Helen?"

"No, Rob. I just got back from a flight."

"You one of those flight attendants?" he asked, awed.

"Yes. And I'm headed for the barracks, not the hangar. That's where I work in between flights."

Rob said, "Isn't the WAVES Barracks just through those trees and across the street?"

"Yes."

"So . . . May I walk you back to your barracks?"

She was too exhausted to make the walk. *But wait a minute, I'm tired, yes, but meeting this boy has been . . . what? . . . exciting? Energizing? Yes, I guess so. Why not? If I drop from exhaustion, he can carry me to the barracks!* Smiling, she said, aloud, "Why not? I'd like that."

Helen was short also, and they made a charming pair as they took off for the path through the trees.

* * *

The next day, which Helen had free from between-flight duties, still on her delegated end-of-a-flight rest time, she went to noon chow, wondering if she would run into Rob Erwin again. *What am I thinking? He's just a baby!* But she looked for him, anyway.

He called her from behind. He had just come off his bus from the hangar. "Helen! I wondered if I'd see you again today."

They fell into the line together at the end of the chow line, outside. Again, the line snaked to the entrance of the chow hall. They chatted from the parking lot, up the steps, and into the chow hall and through the chow line. At the end of that, Rob went to the left and Helen went to the right, where they ate separately again.

They met once more, after finishing eating. Rob walked her to the barracks again.

He asked, "Could we go to the movie together tonight, Helen?"

"Oh, I'm sorry, Rob, I'm on the supernumerary list for the next flight."

"The super-what? he asked.

"The supernumerary is a standby. I have to remain available until the next flight is gone with its full crew. If either of the flight attendants can't make it, then I have to step in, in her or his place."

"Well, then, no problem, as I see it. Could I visit you at your barracks?"

"Sure you could. We have a lounge to be with visitors."

He brightened. "Maybe we'll see each other at the evening chow line. That way, we could walk back to your barracks again, and I could visit you there."

"Don't see why not, Rob."

\* \* \*

Helen and Rob did meet at the chow hall. Afterwards, they spent the entire evening at the WAVES Barracks lounge, talking about everything that came to their minds. She found herself enjoying the re-acquaintanceship tremendously. She was still amazed to have encountered him in the Navy, and that he was a second-class petty officer. She still remembered him best as a freshman in high school.

"You know, Helen, I think about those Study Hall days we had together. I think about them a lot. As you know, while you were a senior, I was a freshman, and you always helped me with my homework."

"Oh, yes. I remember. We weren't supposed to talk in Study Hall, so we whispered. Easy to manage, since we sat next to each other."

"You helped me a lot back then. Sometimes I think I learned more from you than I did from my teachers!"

"Come on, Rob. You jest!"

"No, I mean it." He was no longer grinning. He sobered quickly. "Gosh, Helen, you really were an influence on me back then."

"I had no idea, Rob."

"Believe it." He took her hand. "Well," he said, "it's almost time for lights out. I better get going. I'll have to shower and then climb into my bunk in the dark. It'll be a lot past 'lights out' by then."

"I'm glad I didn't get called to be on that flight I was standing by for," she said. "I wouldn't have missed this visit we've had for anything in the world."

Still holding her hand, he stood up, then reached for her other hand to pull her up from the sofa where they had sat together. She stood up beside him.

There was an awkward moment. He said, finally, "Could I kiss you goodnight, Helen?"

"I'd be disappointed if you didn't!"

He put his hands on her shoulders and kissed her rather sensuously, she thought.

She leaned back to look at him comfortably and said, "Good grief! Where in the world did you learn to kiss like that, Rob?"

He stepped back one step and turned his head aside, blushing. "On Prom Night," he said simply. "Old girl friend. We broke up right after I enlisted. She said she'd never forgive me if I did it."

"What a shame, Rob."

"Oh, I felt bad for awhile. But not anymore. I'm glad we crossed paths, Helen. Really. I am."

She smiled at him, and said, "So am I, Rob." She spoke with feeling.

He kissed her again, this time holding her in his arms.

She thought she would pass out. *Helen, old girl, get your feet back onto the ground! He's just a kid, for Pete's sake! Such a nice kid, though. Such a sweet boy.* "Good night, Rob. Sleep well, even if you do have to stumble into your bunk in the dark."

He laughed. "Holy Smoke," he exclaimed. "They even turn out the lights in the lounge?"

"Yes." She initiated the next kiss.

"I better go," he said quickly. "Good night, Helen. And thanks a million for a really great evening!"

"Good night, Rob."

*Thank YOU, dear boy. I feel reincarnated, or something like that. That wasn't bad at all, kissing a boy four years younger than I am.*

She watched him leave the lounge. She walked to the quarterdeck to watch him go out the door. Then she crossed the quarterdeck and approached the ladder to go onto the second deck.

"Robbing the cradle, Helen?" asked Shirley, grinning from ear to ear, her red hair looking like a halo with the light behind her.

"You bet!" Helen answered. She took a first step, then turned and said, "And don't anybody get in my way!"

Shirley's peals of laughter followed Helen up the ladder. "Helen!" she shouted. "You're such a card!"

Shirley became serious and quiet again. She picked up the phone and dialed the number for the BOQ. She said, "Lieutenant

Albertson, please?"

"I'll ring his room."

"Lieutenant Albertson."

"Jim? It's me."

"Shirl? Something wrong? It's so late!"

"I know. And I apologize. I was hoping you hadn't hit the sack yet."

"I haven't. I'm just out of the shower. If only you could see me now . . ."

"Don't I wish!"

Laughter through the telephone, in both directions. "So, what's up, Hon?"

"Nothing, really. Just wanted to hear your voice. I miss you, Jim, when you're gone on flights. I miss you terribly."

He said, smiling, "Multiply that by a hundred times, and that's how much I miss you, Honey."

"Well, that's all, I guess. Good night, Jim."

"Shirl. Want me to dress and come down to see you? You have a couple more hours on duty."

"Oh, no, I couldn't ask you to do that . . . although now that I think of it, it would be nice . . ."

"Hang in there, Baby. I'll be right over."

* * *

On Shirley's next day off, Saturday, Jim was between flights, and he made a really big date with her. He met her very early in the morning at the WAVES Barracks, and they walked to the bus station on the base, just two blocks from the barracks. They caught an early bus into deecee.

They had breakfast at a White Castle. They slipped into the Smithsonian Museum. They walked up the Capitol steps, sitting on the top step to catch their breath. They took the elevator to the top of Washington Monument and viewed the panoramic view of the city.

They had lunch at a seafood restaurant. They circled the Jefferson Memorial, then made their way to the Lincoln Memorial. They passed the FBI building, and they visited the Treasury Department. They did a quick look at the Supreme Court building. Last, they went to the Library of Congress and viewed the Declaration of Independence with a mixture of awe and reverence. It was like a history lesson and a civics lesson combined, seeing all those parts of the nation's capital. To end the afternoon's informal tour of deecee, Jim took Shirley canoeing on the Potomac. It was frightfully romantic.

Dinner was at a tiny nightclub, the Balalaika. They danced afterward. Jim was a smooth dancer, and a good leader, making it easy for Shirley to follow his subtle signals. She said to herself, *Jim's such a good dancer, he makes me look good!*

Late, very late, they went back to the deecee bus station, stopping at a snack bar next door to buy some sodas and cheese and crackers to have on the bus. They caught the last bus back to the base. It was 2:30 a.m. when the bus dropped them off at the base bus station.

Holding hands, they walked leisurely to the WAVES Barracks. At the bottom step, Jim held her in his arms and murmured into her red hair, "Honey, I never had a more wonderful day in my life."

"Neither did I, Jim. It was heavenly . . . being with you made it that way." Then they kissed.

"Sweetheart, I ache for you every time I go on a flight. I'm always afraid you'll . . ." He was reluctant to finish the thought.

"Afraid I'll what?" she asked.

"It's nothing."

"No," she insisted, "I want to know what you're afraid of. Can't imagine what you're thinking."

He took a deep breath and said, "Afraid you'll meet someone else while I'm gone and . . . I'd lose you, for sure."

"No way, James Albertson! No way!"

They kissed once more. They walked up the steps and onto the porch and kissed one last time.

"Good night, Sweet Knight."

"Good night, Fair Lady."

She went onto the quarterdeck, down the passageway, and into her room. After showering, she climbed into her bed, pulled up the covers, and turned over to go to sleep.

But Shirley Jackson did not sleep. She was too thrilled for words.

* * *

Ginny Gray had been sitting in the lounge, in the semi-darkness, when Shirley slipped through the front door. Not speaking to the MAA on duty, she apparently went straight to her room. Ginny knew that Shirley had had a date with Jim Albertson.

*What a nice thing that Lieutenant Albertson finally gave up pursuing Elizabeth, and what an even greater thing that he turned to Shirley. All that red hair, and his blue-black mop—they make a colorful pair.*

*And what a nice thing, too, that Angie has met a radioman from our own squadron! He's so witty. Must be nice company for her.*

*Helen, after her wild experience in the desert and a sweet parting with a short-term suitor, has found someone to take his place, as it were. A boy from her home town—even the same school. He is so darned cute. Boyish looking, to be sure, but not a boy in spirit, so I'm told. He's a downright Lochinvar!*

*What a thing! Angela goes from a Duke to a first-class petty officer. And Helen goes from an Emir to a second-class petty officer. In both cases, it's Riches to Rags, so to speak.*

*Jean's English RAF friend finally got his assignment to the British Embassy in deecee. What a coup that was for both of them! He's spending every weekend with her—either here at Pax or up in deecee. How wonderful for them!*

*And what about Elizabeth? Frivolous, but always focused, somehow, bent on dating every unmarried officer in the squadron—and that's most of them. Only the Lieutenant Commanders, most of them, are married. Then there are the odd "older-in-years" pilots, who still have the rank of Lieutenant (many of them former enlisted men), and who are married.*

*Then there's Gloria . . . and Sergeant Virgil Blake. Their romance is still raging by correspondence between them. I certainly wish I could meet him. Maybe on my next flight to Germany, I could arrange a meeting . . . no, that wouldn't be seemly. When Gloria's ready to introduce him to the rest of us, that'll be fine. I'm so curious about him, in spite of all the things Gloria has already told me. I wonder what he looks like. Gloria's never produced any snapshots. I wonder.* Ginny sighed a deep sigh, got up from the chair where she had been sitting for hours, and climbed the ladder to get to her cubicle and into her bunk. Tossing and turning during the remainder of the night, she slept fitfully.

\* \* \*

Gloria lay in her upper bunk, wide awake. She had gone to bed early, wanting to be rested before she began a two-weeks' typing project for the Terminal Officer. He had had her removed from the flight scheduling lists, temporarily, so that she could type the horrendous annual report.

That meant that Virgil, newly arrived at his new posting at the Army recruiting office in deecee, could meet her on a weekend day off. Their free days would, happily, coincide.

*I've made up my mind. I'm not going to meet Virgil in deecee and do the town. It's time I introduced him to my shipmates. I'm going to call him tomorrow and tell him to come down to Pax, and we'll figure out what to do after he gets here.*

*I've postponed this event long enough! It's time I take a stand and let everyone know that my Army Sergeant boyfriend is a negro. I dread the shocking looks, the probing questions . . . the everything. But it has to be done!*

*This is my resolve: I will call Virgil tomorrow to invite him to come here and to tell him how to get here. And I will have other things to share with him—like my decision to go off flight status. There. Now I can go to sleep. I think.*

Gloria let the sleep gradually and peacefully overtake her.

# Chapter Seven

Sgt. Virgil Blake took the bus from deecee down to NAS Patuxent River. He was going to visit Gloria. She had already phoned him at his new duty station earlier in the week and told him that this Saturday and Sunday she would have off. She would be working at the terminal for two weeks while she typed up an annual report. After the report was finished, she was going to go off flight status. She would not have to fly again, ever. For her sake, he was glad she had made that decision.

It was Saturday, and they both had the weekend off.

*I can't believe I'm actually going to see her today. It's been so long between sightings, between visits, between the luscious kisses. Ah, the kisses...*

*We have to set a date to get married, absolutely, today! Now that we're stationed this close together, both of us on the East Coast. It's time to set a date. We can work out something for where to live. And if that doesn't pan out, we can always be together on weekends because she said she would be quitting flying after this two-week job is done. Hooray for Gloria!*

*I can't believe I'm making these kinds of plans. It's not set in concrete, however! Not yet.*

*Ah, Gloria, it's going to be so nice to hold you in my arms again and greet you with a hundred kisses!*

His reverie was broken. The bus pulled into the base bus station. The "station" had been much busier during the War. But for now, it was a place to take on and drop off passengers, only a few times a day. There was no ticket agent on duty anymore. The benches, protected by the overhead roof, with no walls, were empty most of the time.

Virgil remembered Gloria's directions for walking to the WAVES Barracks, as she had told him on the phone. He savored the sight of stands of trees—pines and maples, just as Gloria had described—and he grew more impatient as he neared the barracks.

Looking ahead, he said to himself, *That must be the barracks curving street, uphill. More pines and maples all across the back. Oh, yes, Gloria. It's all here, just as you've written in letters and told me on the phone. Here I come, Honey, ready to spend a happy and fabulous two days with you once more.*

Upon entering the WAVE barracks, he took off his hat and placed it under his left arm. Striding up to the MAA desk/counter, he said, "You aren't Shirley, are you? She's supposed to be a redhead."

"That's right, Sergeant. She's off today. I have the weekend duty."

"I see." He looked around, recognizing the description of the quarterdeck, as described by Gloria in one of her letters. The back door, ahead of him. The front door, through which he had just passed, was still in back of him.

Finally, he said, "I've come to see Gloria Thomas. Is she in the barracks right now?"

The MAA looked at him curiously and said, "Well . . . didn't you know?"

"Know what?"

The MAA on duty took a deep breath. "Gloria Thomas was in an accident three days ago. She was killed. . ."

"She what?" His face turned ashen brown. He tossed his hat onto the nearest chair and pushed his fingers across the top of his head.

"That's right. It was a bus/airplane accident. The bus driver approached the crossing of the runway, didn't notice the red light, indicating he should stop. And an aircraft just landing clipped the front of the bus, causing it to flip over twice. Several injuries, but Gloria was the only fatality. Killed outright, the Dispensary doctor surmised. Her funeral was yesterday, in Atlanta. Today, there was a memorial service for her here at Patuxent, in the chapel.

"They've just let out. Several people who went to the service are now in the lounge, right there." She pointed to her left.

Virgil was speechless. He couldn't digest all this information. He had to think. He needed to be alone. He looked at the back door and remembered that from the back door there was a path through the trees to the chapel.

The chapel! A place that Gloria loved. He found his way through the door, down the steps, through the trees, across the parking lot, and into the chapel. The door was not locked.

*Thank God it's open!*

He walked inside, slowly, tears brimming in his eyes. He sat in a pew to the left, a few rows from the front. He rested his forearms on the back of the pew in front of him, clasping his hands in despair. He lowered his head.

He began to sob.

\* \* \*

Ginny Gray left the WAVES Barracks lounge and went to the head. Upon her return to the lounge, passing through the quarterdeck, the MAA stopped her, saying, "Ginny, the darndest thing just happened."

"Like what?"

"An army guy, a sergeant, just walked in, asking for Gloria. He didn't know what had happened to her."

"Did you tell him?"

"Well. Sure. He was a colored man."

Ginny straightened suddenly. "He was?"

"Yeah. What in the world is a colored man doing, asking for Gloria? By the way, that's his hat there on the chair."

"Where is he now?"

"Dunno. He went out the back door."

"To the chapel, do you suppose?"

"Dunno."

Ginny picked up the hat and headed for the chapel. Upon entering it, she saw him sitting there, head bowed. She walked slowly up the aisle, pausing at the pew just behind him. She saw his sergeant's stripes.

She cleared her throat, and then she spoke. "Pardon me, Sergeant . . ."

He raised his head abruptly and turned to see who had spoken to him. A stranger, to be sure, his not knowing another soul on this base.

"Are you Sergeant Virgil Blake?" she asked.

"Yes, but how did you know?"

"I knew it would be you, even before I saw you. Also, I read your rank and name inside your hat." She set it beside him on the pew.

"Of course. And thanks." He turned forward again and bowed his head once more.

Ginny began again. "You just found out about Gloria?"

Virgil nodded.

She said, "I'm so sorry, Sergeant. You must be devastated."

Once more he nodded.

She continued. "I feel as though I know you very well because Gloria shared her thoughts about you . . . a lot!"

His head snapped upward and turned toward her again. "You're Ginny, aren't you?"

"Yes, I am.

"You were Gloria's best friend. She wrote me and told me repeatedly. She valued your friendship very highly, over everyone else."

"Thank you . . . may I call you Virgil?"

Of course, Ginny!"

"Well," she said hesitatingly, "I'll be going now. You may want to be alone for awhile." Her left hand rested on the back of the pew in which he sat.

Reaching around his right side, he put out his left hand to cover hers. "No, Ginny. Please don't go. I need to talk, to remember . . . so much. And still, so little."

Ginny walked back to the aisle and then into the pew where Virgil sat. She sat beside him, his hat between them.

He faced forward again and said, "It's ironic. Gloria was afraid to fly, and what happened to her? She bought it, not *in* an airplane, but *by* an airplane."

Ginny asked, "You knew she was afraid to fly?"

"Mm hm. She told me early on, after we met. She ever talk to you about it?"

"Once in awhile it came up. She didn't dwell on it, however."

"You know, she wrote me some time ago that when she looked at an aircraft, she saw a Bird of Prey. Then, she said, 'It turned into a Bird of Death.' Premonition?"

"Could be, Virgil."

"Again, it's *so* ironic! Her fear of flying. She had no fear of an airplane on the ground . . ."

Ginny said softly, "I know, Virgil."

He went on. "And what's even worse, Ginny. Gloria told me on the phone just this week that after she finishes the two-weeks typing project, she's going to quit flying, especially in view of the fact we're both on the East Coast now. I can't believe what's happened." He bowed his head, as if to say a silent, short prayer.

After a space in time, Ginny said softly, "Incredible."

Virgil sat back in the pew, looked at his watch and said, "I think I should catch the next bus back to Washington."

She said, "There's a schedule posted at the bus station. Want company for the walk to it?"

"I certainly do!"

They walked slowly, talking quietly and mostly about Gloria. Virgil said, "You know, Ginny, Gloria and I discussed marriage, from time to time."

Ginny listened respectfully.

"We especially discussed the problems of a mixed marriage. The difficulties it would bring on. The insults. The snide remarks. It was all bound to happen. But we felt we could weather all that. That we could survive. And look at us now. She's gone, forever. At least there won't be the apprehension about a white woman marrying a negro."

Ginny felt her skin crawl. It had been a shock to discover that Gloria's Sergeant Blake was a man of color. She thought about that.

What were her own feelings about consorting with a man of color? She wasn't sure. But she was sure that she liked this man, soft-spoken, clearly mourning for Gloria, still strong in spirit. It was intriguing.

They arrived at the bus station and read the posted schedule. They sat on a bench in front of the now-unused ticket window. They continued to chat while they waited for the bus.

Virgil said, "You know, Gloria wanted to go to college, after she got out of the Navy—she wasn't in for the 20 years, like me. And I told her that I was 'in college' already, in a manner of speaking. By that I mean that the Education Officer for our unit in Wiesbaden sent for regular Army courses to be mailed to him so that they could be taught to those who were interested.

"I chose Physics and English. Those were two that were offered. The Education Officer taught English. Another officer in the unit, who was a physicist, taught Physics . . . naturally.

"Those of us who finished the courses have received college credits."

Ginny said, "Nice!"

"You bet! And having once tasted the success of it, I want more. I'm signing up for evening classes in deecee at George Washington University."

"Virgil, that's great! Great that you want to improve and add to your education."

"Don't get me wrong, Ginny. There's a motive."

"And that would be?"

"A commission. I want to make officer."

"I see. Ambition is in the formula, isn't it?"

"You bet!"

"Gloria would be proud of you, Virgil."

He sighed. "I had hoped so."

There was a slight pause. Then she said to him, "I sincerely hope, Virgil, that you can get through this loss without too much pain."

"Thanks, Ginny. I'll try. That's all I can do." He looked at her. "You've been a great help, by the way. I'm so glad you came to the chapel. I would have wanted to meet you, eventually, to talk about Gloria . . ."

She squeezed his arm. He put his hand on hers.

He removed his hand. She removed her hand from his arm. He sighed heavily. They waited.

* * *

In the WAVES Barracks lounge, the knot of mourners moved

about aimlessly, making small talk, not knowing where to start—nor where to end.

Wing Cdr. Michael Reid had come down from deecee to be with Jean Trimwood for Gloria's memorial service. Shirley Jackson and Lt. James Albertson were there. Bill Wagner and Rob Erwin joined Angela Rowen and Helen Enasevich for the service.

Wing Cdr. Reid said, above everyone's voice, "Why don't we go somewhere for dinner? My treat."

There were murmurs of agreement and six of the group headed for the door. Michael looked back and noticed that the two U.S. Navy enlisted men were not coming with the others. He went to them and said, "You must come with us. We are all remembering Gloria Thomas together. Ignore the rank differences, just today. Come."

Rob and Bill were impressed . . . and relieved. And they were smiling as they joined the others.

The group was to travel in two cars: Wing Cdr. Reid had purchased an English Austin upon his getting settled in deecee. Recently, Bill Wagner had resurrected a 1939 Packard.

Before they departed the barracks, Shirley asked the MAA on duty where Ginny was. She reported that Ginny left by the back door, and that she thought she was going to the chapel. Then she told about the army sergeant, a colored man, who had asked for Gloria, his not already knowing what had happened to her.

Shirley took in all this and put two and two together.

*An army sergeant? Must be Gloria's boy friend. And he's a negro? Do I have that right?*

Michael and Jean sat in the front of his Austin, Jim and Shirley in the back. Bill and Angela were in his Packard's front seat, Rob and Helen in the back. The two cars took off, caravanning. Bill would lead the way, for he knew how to get to the Esperanza, a seafood restaurant on the Patuxent River, a favorite restaurant of the Navy people from the base.

Helen and Angie noticed Elizabeth Holmes in a car that passed them on their left. They made their usual comments, laughing about Elizabeth's propensity for being with a different officer each time they saw her. Bill and Rob were baffled. The young women told them the story of the now infamous Elizabeth Holmes. The men offered their smiles, without comments. Helen and Angie continued shrieking with laughter.

In Michael Reid's car, Jean and Shirley had also noticed Elizabeth's passing them.

"Okay. Let's have it," Jean said. "Who is Elizabeth with this time?"

Shirley said, "Darned if I know."

And Jim said, "Darned if I care!" He squeezed Shirley's hand, tightly, and shared a smile with her.

They began laughing, all except Michael. He was nonplussed and asked why they were laughing. They explained. He joined in the merriment, a relief, for all of them, from the somberness of the day.

* * *

While Ginny and Virgil sat side-by-side on the bus station bench, he said to her, "Thank you so much, Ginny, for being here with me. I do appreciate it a lot. You're everything Gloria wrote about."

"And so are you, Virgil. Everything." She took his hand in hers.

For the first time since hearing the tragic news about Gloria, he smiled.

They heard the bus approach. The air brakes were applied with a light screech. The bus had stopped behind them. Two passengers, enlisted men, alighted and, with ditty bags in hand, walked to the nearest street corner to catch a station bus to take them to their barracks.

Virgil stood up, Ginny still holding his hand. He bent down and kissed her on the forehead. "Thank you again, Ginny, for so much."

"You're welcome, Virgil." She paused, still holding his hand, and continued. "I truly hope to see you again, soon."

He smiled again. She released his hand. He straightened up and walked to the open door of the bus, leaving her behind him.

Ginny remained seated, her back to the bus, shoulders slightly slumped. She felt terrible. A terrible loss. Her friend Gloria. And now, she felt as if she were losing Virgil. *How could I think I'm losing Virgil? I never had him, for heaven's sake!*

The bus door closed with a soft hissing sound. It backed out of its loading/unloading space. It traveled toward the back of the station, turned right, went across the back of the station, turned right again, and traveled back toward the main street.

Before it headed for the main street, after its last turn around the bus station, the Packard and Austin pulled into the parking area on that side of the bus station.

Everyone had seen Ginny sitting on the bench, alone. They decided to stop and bring her with them. She needed cheering up, perhaps more than the others, for they all knew that she and Gloria had been close friends.

While they were climbing out of the cars, and the bus passed behind them, on its way out, they saw a lone figure standing where the bus had been parked. They didn't know who it was.

After the bus had turned back onto the main street and disappeared, Ginny turned to her left to look at what she thought would be an emptiness. But there stood the lone figure, watching her. She knew who it was.

It was Sergeant Virgil Blake.

# BOOK TWO

1950 - 1992

# Chapter Eight

In the Esperanza Restaurant, Virgil Blake and Ginny Gray sat across from each other at the long, narrow table. Whenever Virgil glanced toward Ginny, he found her looking at him—not staring, but looking at him. Meanwhile, he listened to the conversations around him: Gloria was a tireless worker; she was loyal to the Naval service; and her southern accent and manners were her most endearing charms.

There, Virgil noticed, was Ginny looking at him again—or was it yet? It did not make him uncomfortable, but he was becoming more curious about the behavior as the evening wore on.

Wing Commander Michael Reed, seated at the head of one end of the table, said to Virgil who was seated two chairs to his right, "Sergeant, I understand you've recently been transferred to the Army recruiting office in Washington."

"Yes, sir," replied Virgil.

"Do you live in the city? Or Virginia, or Maryland?"

"I live in deecee, sir. I share an apartment with three Army buddies—men I've known from elsewhere in the Army."

Ginny thought, *He's saying "deecee," just like the rest of us in the squadron. Probably picked it up from Gloria.*

Michael continued, "When we're finished here and take the others back to the base, could I give you a lift to your apartment? I live in the city, also."

"Why, yes, sir. That would be very helpful. Thank you very much, sir."

Jean Trimwood said, "Michael, I'd really like to go back to the barracks early. Ginny and I have a flight tomorrow morning. It's been a stressful day."

"So it has," Michael acknowledged. He motioned for the check.

Shortly afterward, the group left the restaurant, and once again they traveled in the two cars. Michael and Helen in Michael's Austin, with Jim Albertson and Shirley Jackson riding in the back seat. Bob Wagner and Angela Rowen in his Packard's front seat; Helen Enasevich and Rob Erwin in the back seat, with Virgil next to Helen, and once again Ginny was on Virgil's lap, the same arrangement as when they traveled from the base bus station to the restaurant.

Ginny had mixed feelings about sitting on his lap. It seemed unduly intimate. But nice. She felt she might be blushing. *Ninny! Enjoy the moment!* And she did.

When the two cars arrived at the WAVES barracks, everyone alighted; they all said their goodbyes to each other, thanking Michael for the dinner; some kissing going on.

Virgil and Ginny stood beside the Packard. He said to her, "We didn't get to talk very much this evening. Actually, not at all."

"Regrettable," she responded.

"I hope to be able to fix that. I hope to see you after your next flight."

"I hope so, too, Virgil, on both counts."

"I still have your barracks phone number, from Gloria."

"Don't lose it!"

"I won't. I promise." He picked up both her hands and held them lightly.

"Good bye, Sergeant."

"Oh, Ginny, don't say 'good bye. "Say 'good night,' please."

"All right, then. Good night, Virgil."

With a gentle squeeze of her hands, he said, "Good night, Ginny. Again, I thank you for being there in the chapel with me. I feel so much better about . . . everything."

She smiled at him, which he could see quite well from the light next to the barracks door, shining onto her face. He smiled back to her.

"Ready, Sergeant Blake?" asked Commander Reid.

"Yes, sir. Coming right away, sir."

\* \* \*

Jean said to Ginny during the return flight from the Azores to Westover AFB, "You're awfully quiet, Ginny—for the entire trip. Something amiss?"

"Yes and no."

"And that means?"

"I've been thinking a lot about Sergeant Blake. I feel so sorry for him, his losing Gloria."

"We all feel sorry for him."

"I'm sure," she said with a light sigh.

Upon entering the barracks, at the end of the last leg of their flight, Shirley handed Ginny a telephone message. It was from Sergeant Blake.

It said, "Ginny, please call me as soon as you return to Pax." The message then included his phone numbers, at work and at his apartment.

Ginny went to the pay phone, in one corner of the quarterdeck and called him.

"Sergeant Blake, please."

"Just a moment."

"Sergeant Blake speaking."

"Virgil! It's Ginny."

"You're back? Safely? I'm glad. Ginny, I want to see you. I *must* see you. As soon as possible!"

"Of course!"

They met in deecee the next afternoon, at the end of Virgil's Saturday duty. They went to dinner.

"So," Ginny began, after they had ordered, "what's up, Sergeant? What is so urgent that you have to see me so soon?"

"Honey . . . If I may call you that?"

"Oh, please do!"

"Thanks. Gin . . . and may I call you that, too?"

"Of course! My father calls me that all the time. It was he who gave me the name 'Ginny' instead of 'Virginia.'" *I love it when my dad calls me 'Gin.' I love it that Virgil has begun doing it, too.* "Gloria used to call me Gin, as well."

Hearing that about Gloria gave him a tug, but he continued. "Gin, I thought about you all the time since we said good night at your base."

"And?"

"And . . . I want to be with you every chance we can get! Can we do that, Ginny?"

"I don't see why not. In fact, I'd be proud to be with you every opportunity that comes along."

"Then it's settled. Just like with Gloria . . ." He paused. "Oh, I didn't mean to say that. That didn't come out right."

"No. But go on. What did you mean to say?"

Virgil, with his guard up now, said, "I mean that I'd like to maintain a friendship with you, just as I did with Gloria—meeting every time we have the same days off."

"That's sweet, Virgil. I wish the same. I'd be honored to see you and be with you every time our schedules permit it."

\* \* \*

Virgil maintained his warm memories of Gloria by connecting with Ginny, who was Gloria's best friend. They met in deecee; they ate in restaurants; they went to movies; they went dancing; and they went sightseeing. They met at the base; they ate in the civilian cafeteria; they went to the movies; they went bowling; they went dancing, whenever there was a dance on the base; and they went on scheduled Navy boat rides across the Patuxent River onto Solomons Island and return.

Solomons had a USO, a movie house, and a restaurant. It was a very small fishing village on an island off the end of a peninsula, connected by a 20-foot causeway. The peninsula was bordered on the west by the Patuxent River and on the east by the Chesapeake Bay.

Even when Ginny was gone on a five-to-seven-day flight, Virgil wrote letters to her (just as he had to Gloria). She sent him postcards from abroad, hunting for out-of-the-way post offices for the various foreign stamps.

The friendship flourished. It was heady. For both of them.

Ginny's shipmates, the other female flight attendants, noticed a change in her: a glow, one said; subdued, but not cowed, said another; and definitely prettier than they'd ever seen her before, declared others.

Ginny would have been surprised to hear that last comment. Perhaps she would not have believed it. But she would have liked it, anyhow. Being a Plain Jane had dogged her opinion of herself all her life. Indeed, the comment about being pretty would have been incomprehensible, to her.

In 1951, when Ginny was 28 years old, her second Navy enlistment was up. Just before being discharged, she and Virgil were having dinner at a favored seafood restaurant in deecee.

She began, "Virgil, I'm going to be discharged from the Navy next month, and I've made plans for my future."

This was shocking news to him, "Plans? You have plans for the future?" he asked.

"Well, yes. I've applied for entrance to the University of Kansas and have been accepted. A room at the dorm is waiting for me to move in, when I get there. As you know, I already have two years of college behind me. I need two more years to get a degree and a teaching certificate."

Virgil exploded at the news! "You what? Why can't you matriculate right here at Georgetown University? Why in the devil do you have to go to Kansas!?"

"Virgil, people are looking at us. Let's take a walk and thrash this out later."

He paid the check, and they left. He had cooled down a bit as they left the restaurant. But she asked, "Why are you so hostile about this, Virgil?"

"Because, my dear, *I* have plans, too. For me. And for us."

She held her breath. *For us? What in the world does that mean?* She decided to articulate her thought. "For us? What in the world does that mean?"

They had reached a city park and sat down on the nearest park bench. He said, "It means, my darling, that someday, down the road, I want us to get married. There! I said it!"

Ginny thought herself to be a person who was not into histrionics, but surely this was such an occasion. Maybe.

"Well," he said, "what do you say about that?"

"I'm thinking."

"You don't want us to get married? Down the line? If not, I can understand . . . my being a negro."

"Oh, yes, indeed I do want us to get married, Virgil. You'll never know how much! Your being negro is not an issue. Not in the least bit."

"So?"

"So, I want to have the degree and teaching certificate in my pocket before I marry. You or anyone else."

"And why is that so important? Getting a degree and a teaching certificate, with a marriage in the offing."

"In case my spouse should die unexpectedly, early in life, I'd need something to fall back onto right away. Teaching could be the answer. Teachers are always in demand. Everywhere!"

He took a deep breath, then expelled it. He was unable to speak.

"Besides," she went on. "You have a very dangerous occupation, in the event of another war. And, historically, there will be more wars. Count on it. You could lose your life in a war, heaven forbid. I could face a young and long widowhood."

He toyed with his lapel. He looked up at her and said, "You know, you're right. It could happen exactly as you say."

She turned the subject back onto him. "You said earlier that you have plans for yourself, too. What are they?"

He took another deep breath, preparing himself for the long speech. "As you know, Gin, I've been taking classes, both in Wiesbaden and here in deecee. Furthermore, I've been challenging courses right and left, passing their final exams, and getting credits for every class I've challenged. Also, for every Army course I've taken, I get credits for that, too. In 1952, next year, I'll be receiving my degree. Immediately upon getting it, I'll be completing my request for assignment to Officer Candidate School."

"Virgil! That's wonderful! And, I remember your talking about getting a commission—the first time we met." She was interested in hearing that he was still bent on becoming an officer.

"Yeah, well, don't count on anything just yet. I still have to gather up the rest of the required recommendations, as well as actually graduate from college!"

"But it's still wonderful!"

"Right. Officer Candidate School, takes 14 weeks. Then I have to do a ground-officers' training school."

"I'll be graduating," she offered, "in 1953. Then I begin a one-year practice teaching time, in Kansas, of course."

"Good lord! Another delay?" The wheels of his mind were spinning. *Maybe, after all the schooling, I can get assigned for duty at Ft. Riley. That's in Kansas. Gotta work on that!*

Gradually, their plans and their schedules were finalized. She asked him, to proceed in a pleasant conversation, "So what classes are you taking currently?"

"Math. Lots of math."

"Why so much math?"

"For an electronics engineering degree."

"I'm impressed!"

"I am, too." They grinned at each other. He put his arms around her shoulders. They shared a warm kiss.

For the moment, they were both at peace. A future had been outlined. It was an agreeable arrangement. For both of them.

*   *   *

And according to their plan, Virgil received his degree, made it to OCS, got his commission, did the ground-officer training, and got transferred to Fort Riley, Kansas (by design, rather than by coincidence—his design).

They were able to see each other often throughout 1952 and 1953. During that time, they had a date in Kansas City, Missouri, where they re-visited the World War I Memorial. They chose a bench to sit on.

Thoughtfully, they regarded their surroundings. Virgil spoke with an off-the-wall question: "Gin, about when did you learn that I am a negro?"

"What?" she asked, distractedly.

"I asked, about when did you learn that I am a negro?"

"Ah. You caught me off guard. I was thinking about the WWI veterans—how many are there?—where are they?—what are they doing these days?—but this is not answering your question."

"True."

She went on. "Well, Gloria never told us you were a man of color. But she did announce, just before she was killed, that you were coming to the base that weekend, and that she was going to introduce you to everyone!"

"So then she did tell you about me?"

"No. I discovered it when I talked to the MAA on duty, on the day of her memorial service at the chapel. The MAA told me that 'an Army sergeant, a negro,' had asked for Gloria. She told me also that you hadn't known about Gloria's death."

"So, you knew it was I she was referring to?"

"Yes. I put the facts together and came to that conclusion. Of course, when I picked up your hat, I saw your rank and name on the inside of it. And when I followed you to the chapel and saw you there, I knew for sure it was you."

"So you brought me my hat, sat and talked a bit, then walked me to the base bus station."

"Yes," she said. "Then the bus pulled out of the station. And to my surprise and utter delight, I turned and saw you standing where the bus had been. You never boarded it."

"That's right. And then your friends asked us to join them for dinner."

She nodded. He went on. "It must've been an enormous shock to you, finding out about my being negro only after Gloria died."

"It was a shock, all right. But not enormous. As soon as you spoke in the chapel, and after our talk on the way to the base bus station, and at the bus station, I could sense you were everything Gloria had told me about you. I liked you instantly. You weren't on guard, you were warm and compassionate. You spoke well. Your talk was engaging. I really liked you, Virgil."

She paused, then continued. "I was even hoping, in that first meeting, that you liked me . . ."

"Oh, Honey, I did! I did!" He put an arm around her shoulders. "I really did! But I held back in the very beginning, thinking about Gloria, not wanting to sully my memories of her."

"Of course," she said. "I even felt a pang of disloyalty, letting myself like you as much as I did—from the beginning."

"It's passed now? The feeling of disloyalty?"

"Yes. And you? What about your feelings about Gloria?"

"I'll always remember her, of course, but my heart is in your hands now, dear one."

Because it was a public place, they kissed one another with restraint. Later, when she said goodbye to him at the Kansas City bus station, they kissed again, this time with greater feeling. A huge wave of relief and another welcomed wave of contentment washed over both of them.

\* \* \*

Ginny graduated in 1953, and they were married the same day. Her parents came from New Mexico. Virgil had one aunt, a couple of uncles, and some cousins, all in Toledo. Only the aunt came to the wedding.

Virgil's Aunt Etta was apprehensive about being among so many white people, at a formal affair. *Poor boy,* she thought. *Losin' his mamma while he's so young. Never knowin' his daddy. I hope this marriage works out good for him. They look happy. For now. The boy is mighty handsome in his fancy uniform. His mamma'd be so proud. I'm so proud.*

\* \* \*

They honeymooned in Kansas City, Missouri, her practice teaching stint in Kansas City, Kansas, looming on Monday. They spent most of the time in each other's arms.

She watched him sleeping the next morning, beside her. *Never in a million years would I have dreamed I could be this happy....deliriously happy. Never could I have wished for a more attentive, sweet, loving husband and lover. I'm so lucky! So raving, wildly lucky.*

She drifted back to sleep, while Virgil slept on, a faint smile on his face, possibly dreaming.

\* \* \*

Virgil rounded a corner in the hallway of the maternity ward. It was the second time he was going to view his son. A doctor approached, while Virgil looked with awe at the tiny bundle in his cart/bed.

The doctor asked, "You're Lieutenant Blake, aren't you?"

"Yes, sir." Virgil looked up.

"I'm Dr. Bryant. I delivered your baby boy yesterday."

"Yes, sir. My wife told me."

"I'm afraid I have some bad news for both of you. I told Mrs. Blake earlier this morning, and you need to know now that your wife cannot have any more children."

Virgil was shocked and wanted to know why that was so.

"There were complications during the delivery. She should not get pregnant again. There are two ways to manage that: one, surgery for her; two, a vasectomy for you. Talk it over, take your time, and let us know what you decide."

Trying to fathom what the doctor had just told him, he excused himself hastily and hurried to Ginny's room.

"Gin! Gin, Gin," he cried out.

"You know?" she asked.

"I just found out. Oh, sweetheart, what're we going to do?"

She was unable to answer him. She wept, heartbroken.

He put his arms around her and wept with her.

The next day, they took little Eddie (named for Virgil's middle name, Edward) to his first home. They got him settled into the crib in his room. They sat down on the sofa in the living room and discussed, pro and con, the problem that lay at the bottom of their hearts.

She said to him, "If you should have a vasectomy, and I should predecease you, and you should marry a child-bearing-aged woman, you would want to have more children. But that wouldn't be possible."

"That's right."

"And although surgery for me is more complex, requiring a longer recovery than for you, after a vasectomy, at least *you* could have more children."

"Right again."

"Then is it settled?"

"Darling, I hate like the devil to have you go through any more than what's already been done!"

"But I'm willing, Virgil. For you, sweetheart."

"I'll take leave and stay at home to look after you and the baby both. Gin, you're the greatest! I love you so much."

"Oh, darling, I love you. You're the most, the best.

"I was thinking last night, in the clinic," she went on. "And I want us to adopt two more children. We're probably getting too old to get babies. We could adopt two older children. Girls are what I'd like. Sisters, if we could."

She paused, looking at him. "Mixed blood."

"Of course!" he exclaimed. "Darling, whatever you want, I want, too."

They hugged each other.

He said, "We'll be transferring to Fort Sheridan, Illinois, in another few months. We'll begin the adoption application as soon as we get there. I'll bet we can find exactly what you want. You'll see."

"I can hardly wait!"

\* \* \*

In late 1954, the transfer to Fort Sheridan went smoothly, even with an infant in tow. They were so happy. . . and thankful that they at least had this first baby. The adoption process began.

By 1956 two little sisters, mixed blood (as Ginny and Virgil had wished), joined the Blake family, permanently. Monica was 6, and

Annabel was 5. They were from Chicago.

"Annie," said Ginny, "do you want some more homemade soup?"

"No'm."

"It's mamma, Annie. You can call me mamma, now. All the time."

"Yes'm. I mean . . . mamma?"

"Yes, darling. Mamma."

Annie, home from morning kindergarten class, could hardly wait for Monica to arrive home that day, from first grade.

She rushed outside to greet her big sister. "Monica, Monica! We have a mamma! We can call her mamma now!"

\* \* \*

In 1965 Virgil came home at the end of the day, from his post in Fort Ord, California, and said, "Well, Honey, I'm long overdue for an overseas assignment, and this is it."

Vaguely, with hands deeply into dishwashing suds, Ginny asked, "To where?"

"Place called Viet Nam."

"I've been reading about that in the newspaper."

"Yeah. I know."

She asked, "Weren't the French embroiled in a war there? And they left?"

"Yeah. I think so."

"Well, we're not at war, per se, are we?"

"Yes and no. Shouldn't amount to much, perhaps."

"Lord, I hope so!"

\* \* \*

Captain Blake served three 18-month tours in Nam, as it eventually came to be called. Although he was only 40 years old when he went on his first tour, the men under him referred to him as "Pappy." Not to his face, of course, but he knew about it early on. He sensed that the term Pappy was a perverted form of respect. That pleased him. So, when they did call him "Pappy," behind his back, he loved it.

Virgil received a Purple Heart during the second tour. However, he refused to wear it, even on formal occasions, declaring to Ginny that it was just a "band-aid" wound. In reality, it was much more serious. He simply neglected to tell her all about it.

More medals were added to his collection. His record reflected deeds of courage time and time again. When, at the end of his last tour, Ginny saw the collection on his chest, for his retirement ceremony in 1972, she realized how little she knew about what really had happened to him in Nam. And when she thought about it, she knew equally little about what really had happened to him in World War II.

Perhaps, she thought, he would reveal more to her about his exploits, eventually. Just perhaps.

Wartime promotions come fast in all the military services. Arriving in Nam as a Captain, Virgil soon moved on to Major. Then, Lieutenant Colonel was his rank at retirement.

The year that Virgil retired from the Army, after 30 years of service, Eddie got appointed to West Point at age 18. Eddie knew all about his father's experiences, in both wars. He admired him enormously. It was a strong influence toward his decision to try for West Point. Virgil had told things to his son that he could never bring himself to tell Ginny. The stories were too gruesome.

After receiving high grades all through school, Eddie garnered recommendations to the Point. His father's having served valiantly and honorably in both World War II and Vietnam helped, in the appointment process. He chose the infantry. His mother was fearful. His father was proud.

\* \* \*

Monica and Annabel, upon their high school graduations, went to college. Monica attended for three years; Annabel for two. Upon completion of their last semesters, they reported to Lisbon, Portugal as church missionaries.

They both married other American missionaries in Lisbon. One was a preacher, and he and Monica were assigned to a small congregation in Minnesota. Annabel's husband became a professor of philosophy at Pepperdine University, Malibu, California.

\* \* \*

Gradually, almost imperceptibly, Virgil noticed the changes in society. The thing he took notice of more than all the others was that Americans began referring to Negroes as "blacks" or "African Americans" or "Afros." Upon reflection, he never felt bad about being called Negro—only the way some people pronounced it. That was demeaning, to his ears.

Also, the children seemed to bear no cross for being half white and half black. They were a curiosity, something to be asked about in a friendly way. They were not put down nor shunned. They seemed to fit in, to be accepted. And Virgil was happy, indeed, to see that happen in his children's lives. All of them were so terribly lucky. Uncommonly lucky, he thought.

Maybe it was just luck. It could have been disastrous in another world, another time. He heaved a long sigh of relief, for his and Ginny's children.

* * *

What to do, after retirement? Virgil had it all mapped out. He even began thinking about retirement while in and out of Nam. They retired in Denver, Colorado. He attended a photography school and later set up a photo studio. Within a year, he was able to hire an assistant. The next year, he hired two assistants.

Ginny began teaching full time when their youngest, Eddie, reported to West Point. After her retirement, at age 55, she was free to tutor young students in the city, those whose backgrounds left much to be desired. She tutored in all subjects, but mostly math and English.

Virgil's photography work was now in demand. He hadn't slowed down. He was only 48 years old; Ginny was 47. Their lives were full of vitality and vigor. They looked back on the years they had been together with fondness and utter satisfaction. The following years were blissful and productive.

Until 1992 when Virgil, at age 70, died. Heart attack.

Ginny, through the strength from her children, carried on. The grandchildren were a joy and kept her life from *ever* being empty.

Each night, however, her bed was now half empty.

# Chapter Nine

Although the dinner party at Esperanza had begun on a somber note, everyone thinking about the loss of Gloria Thomas, conversation picked up eventually. They talked about Gloria, in a lighter vein. Her southern accent, for example, set the tone for some merriment.

Jean Trimwood, seated at Wing Commander Michael Reid's right, caught his eye and smiled at him. Michael smiled back, immensely pleased with the way things were going between them.

After he arrived for attaché duty in D.C., he found an English-style house near Embassy Row. The wife of his young aide served as his hostess whenever he had to entertain in his home officially. Assisting with the arrangements at Commander Reid's home was an additional burden for the aide.

Michael needed a wife! It was too much to expect of the young couple, to be available at every official dinner at Michael's house. It was enough that the aide spent so many hours arranging larger functions at the embassy.

*I need a wife!* he almost said aloud. While listening to conversations around him, he composed a speech that he wanted to say to Jean Trimwood. She had captured his heart (and his sister's and brother-in-law's hearts) back in London. Her college work included a minor in Home Economics. A plus, he decided. He was 32 years old. It was time.

The dinner passed pleasantly enough, in spite of its subdued beginning. Michael offered Sergeant Blake a ride into deecee after delivering the women to their barracks. He accepted.

At the WAVES Barracks, Jean and Michael got out of his car and said good night to each other. "Before you go, Jean, let me tell you that I want to see you as soon as you return from tomorrow's flight. It's important."

"Well, now you have my curiosity aroused. What's up?"

"Not now, m'dear. And not here. I want us to be alone and unhampered by the crush of extra people. Call me as soon as you get back, and we'll make a date."

"Righto, Michael." She had picked up on his favorite response. "Will do!" She kissed him soundly. "Good night, my English Knight."

He smiled. "Good night, Fair Lady."

She ran up the steps and into the barracks.

"Ready, Sergeant Blake?" he called out to Virgil.

"Yes, sir. Coming right away, sir."

* * *

When Jean returned from her flight with Ginny, Ginny used the pay phone as soon as she got her message from Virgil. Jean waited, somewhat impatiently, for she was still thinking mostly about Michael's mysterious date that he wanted to make. He had given her not one clue!

Finally the pay phone was available. "May I speak to Commander Reid? This is Jean Trimwood calling."

"Yes, ma'am. One moment, please."

"Commander Reid here." The telephone receptionist had not given him Jean's name—only "A woman calling you, sir."

"Michael, I'm back."

"Ah, Jean! Thank goodness! I've been on pins and needles, waiting for your call. You have two days off, after the flight. Correct?"

"Correct."

"Darling, I know you're tired, and need to rest, but could you possibly catch a bus immediately, and I'll meet you at the station in the city?"

"For you, Michael, I can do anything . . . almost, that is."

"Jean! You're cheeky! But we've been through that before, haven't we? I'm looking at the bus schedule now. Can you make the 4:30 bus leaving the base? You should have time to shower and change."

"Well, it's a tight squeeze. But I'll be on it!"

"Excellent! I'll see you in the Washington station. I'm so glad you're back, darling. I can hardly wait to see you."

"You make me feel so good, Michael. See you in a little while."

"Righto, m'dear."

* * *

They went to a quiet and elegant restaurant for dinner. They ordered. They gave up their menus. The waiter disappeared. Michael looked at her long and searchingly. He had practiced his speech over and over, dozens of times, while he waited for her return from her last flight.

Somehow, he felt uneasy, the speech half forgotten. It was a big step that he was about to take. He was so nervous! Winifred was the only other woman he had ever proposed to. And to what end? She married someone else!

His hands were sweating.

Jean looked at him worriedly. He appeared to be distressed. "Michael, what is it? Are you all right?"

"No, not all right. I'm as nervous as a cat on hot coals."

She leaned forward in her chair. "Darling! Whatever is it with you tonight?"

"I need a wife!"

"I beg your pardon? You need . . . what?"

"Jean, I'm sorry. I blurted it out in spite of my best-laid plans to make a flowery and acceptable proposal of marriage to you. And I blew it!"

"Oh, no, darling. You didn't blow it. I think what you did and what you said were absolutely charming . . . if I may borrow one of your expressions."

"I didn't blow it?"

"Of course not . . . because, however you said it, 'I need a wife?' I will take on that job! With great pleasure and anticipation......if that's what is being offered....."

"Precisely, m'dear!"

"Oh, Michael, darling, you've made me the happiest woman in the world."

He sighed perceptibly. He smiled. "We should seal it with a kiss, don't you think?"

"I think so. Absolutely."

The table was round and very small. They leaned across it toward each other. He quickly wiped his perspiring hands on his trousers, and he reached for both of her hands. They kissed each other tentatively. It was a far reach, even at the small table.

"Well," he said, leaning back against his chair again. He tried desperately to calm himself. "Well!" he said again. "That makes it official."

"Yes. Well. . . ."

"Darling!" he cried. "I almost forgot—in the heat of forgetting my beautiful speech—" He reached into his pocket, withdrew a small box and placed it before her.

A smile spread across her face. *The dear man procured a ring while I was gone. I guess he got it while I was gone. Naw, he couldn't have bought it <u>before</u> I left. Could he? Why in the world am I questioning the when? Why don't I just reach out for the little box, open it up, and . . . . . .*

She picked up the box and opened it. She gasped. It was the most unusual engagement ring she had ever seen. *What a sparkler!*

"Michael, this is too grand for words. I've never seen anything like it."

"It was my grandmother's. Abigail has our mother's ring, and our mother gave me her mother's."

"Oh, Michael, darling, this is too precious to give to someone else."

"No, it isn't. Not if I'm giving it to someone who is precious to me. That's you, Jean. The jewel of my life. Try it on."

She hesitated, admiring it some more. Then she slipped it onto her finger, and it fit perfectly. "Oh, Michael, I'll treasure this with my life!"

He brought her left hand across the table and leaned into it, kissing first her fingers, then the ring, then her opened hand, on the palm. "I love you with all my soul, Jean, dearest."

The moment was filled with happiness. "And I love you, Michael, my true love."

* * *

They were married in the Navy chapel at Pax in 1950. Jean immediately put in for discharge from the Navy by reason of marriage. Within six weeks, she moved out of the barracks and into Michael's house in deecee.

"Now, this is *our* house, darling," he said. "I hope you like it."

"Michael, I love it. I'd love anything that was yours. Even your lowliest pots and pans in the kitchen!"

"Jean! What is it I've heard your shipmates say about you? You're too much?"

"That's what they say."

* * *

Before the wedding, they had planned their family: two children, right away, because of their ages. Michael said, "If one is a boy, we'll register him at birth to start boarding school at my little alma mater in England when he's nine."

"You'll what? Send our boy off to school at *that* age?"

"Of course. I was! And young Michael III will do the same. It's been done for two generations before him."

"Oh, Michael, we have to discuss this seriously."

"And why does it have to be . . . seriously?"

"Because, my dear, you may as well know, here and now, that I do <u>not</u> consent to send a boy of nine off to England to a boarding school!"

Michael couldn't believe his ears. *This is unheard of. I had no idea an American woman would object to a tradition like this! What's to be done about it?*

She continued, "Besides, if you continue to be military attaché in first one country and then another and another and so on, *that* will be an education unmatched by any school or university anywhere in the world. Rewarding, enriching, challenging; learning new languages and new cultures; exposure to all kinds of people and learning how to relate to them, how to interact with them.

"Darling," she declared, "you are about to provide the greatest kind of education possible for a boy or a girl! . . . just by serving as a military attaché."

He thought, *I never looked at it that way. And she's probably right! How can I get out of doing what's been done for generations in my family?* "You make a lot of sense, Jean. And I agree with your assessment of military attaché postings. But what in heaven's name am I going to tell my family?"

She smiled. "Same things I just said. Of course dear. . . it's your life . . ."

He smiled back, with a mixed bag of uneasiness and relief.

It was settled. He thought, *Close shave! Our first big argument, and we're not even married yet!*

She thought, *'Gad, I hope I wasn't TOO forceful. But the idea did get my dander up! Whew! Glad that's over! Was that our first real argument? I think so.*

* * *

When they married in 1950, he was 32 years old, and she was 30.

Their daughter Beth (Michael's mother's name) was born in 1952, while they were posted to Paris. By the time they left Paris, two years later, Beth, at her tender age, was bi-lingual, a natural.

Their son Michael III was born in Tokyo in 1955, while they were stationed there. By the time they left Tokyo in 1958, both children knew the Japanese language well enough to converse with Japanese children at school, with embassy servants, and with all kinds of shopkeepers.

Their next posting was Bonn, West Germany, from 1959 to 1962. Again, the children learned still another new language, fitting into the local scenes as comfortably as natives.

Greek was their next challenge, in Athens, from 1963 to 1966. Then New Delhi from 1967 to 1970. Michael's last posting, from 1971 to 1974 was in Buenos Aires.

Jean, throughout all these transfers to exotic places, thrived on it. She enjoyed being Michael's hostess at the required functions. She reveled in the children's language skills. She never tired of the breaking up housekeeping and moving on to the next duty. She took great pleasure in setting up a house in each new city, incorporating local objects and furnishings to make each home comfortable and attractive.

They vacationed to England between the first two postings, and they vacationed to America between the next set of postings. Then in England and next to America, and so on.

At the end of the Buenos Aires duty, in 1974, Michael was 56 years old. That was the year he retired.

In the meantime, Beth had finished two years of college in Switzerland. She completed the next two in America, securing a job after graduation at the United Nations as an interpreter. She married an American in 1977, another interpreter at the UN. They had met at an outdoor plaza at the UN at lunchtime. He asked her if he could join her at her table. They were both brown baggers. That was their beginning.

Michael III graduated from Oxford University in 1977, studying international law, after which he signed up with England's Foreign Service. His career was similar to his father's, except for the military connection. His having lived in so many different countries served him well in his career. He married an English girl during his first posting in the Foreign Service. They met at an Embassy party in Rome.

Michael and Jean settled down permanently in a house in West Suffolk County in England. Michael began teaching English and math in an exclusive boys' school in the village. He was an apt teacher. He was entertaining as he regaled the boys with stories of happenings around the world. They soaked up every word he said to them. He loved it. And the boys loved it.

Jean found a new and different life in England, once they settled there. They became members of the local Church of England. She joined a garden club, she formed a book club, she played Bridge once a week, and she and Michael attended small musicales in the nearby city of Ipswich. They attended plays, musicals, and operas in London on a regular basis, staying overnight in a hotel. They renewed the passions of their earliest love for each other.

* * *

Their life in the English countryside was idyllic, a huge change from the hectic moves from one foreign capital city to another. It was a welcome respite. They thrived on it every day. Their health was good. The children were settled into their lives comfortably. Life was grand. Jean thanked God for it all.

# Chapter Ten

When the Navy group finished dinner at the Esperanza Restaurant, W/Cdr Michael Reid paid the check, and everyone prepared to leave.

Shirley Jackson joined Jim Albertson in the back seat of Michael's English Austin for the return trip to the base. They held hands. They conversed now and then with Jean and Michael, who were in the front seat. It was easy to do in a smaller car.

Upon their arrival at the WAVES Barracks, Shirley and Jim alighted. Standing behind the Austin, they hugged one another. He held on to her tightly, whispering into her ear, "Darling, I'm going to miss you something fierce when I leave on my next flight, day after tomorrow."

"I know, Honey. I'll miss you too." They dropped their arms. She continued, "Seems like that's all we ever say to each other anymore. Good grief! What if I were a flight attendant? We'd never see each other! Maybe."

"I don't even want to think about it!"

They kissed with sweet passion.

"Good night, darling," she said.

"Good night, dearest."

*　*　*

While Jim flew to the Azores, to England, back to the Azores, and back to Pax, he had made up his mind what to do upon his return to the base. In fact, it was in England he made his decision. And a purchase.

The first thing he did, after alighting from the plane at Pax, was to go into the terminal and call Shirley. She had just come on duty.

"Sweetheart," he said.

"Jim! You're back! I'm so glad!"

"Shirl. Honey. I'm coming there to talk to you as soon as you get off at midnight. I'll wait for you on the quarterdeck. We can use the lounge, can't we?"

"It'll be dark in the lounge."

"So what? More romantic that way."

"Indeed!"

On the day before his last previous flight, Jim purchased a 1949 DeSoto and was now free from being a slave to the bus schedule. It would take him some time to become accustomed to the new freedom, he surmised. He caught himself studying the bus schedule to figure out where he should be and when. Then he remembered: *Oh, yes, I have my own wheels now!*

He became impatient, waiting for the midnight hour. He arrived at the quarterdeck a full 15 minutes early. Shirley was not busy—rarely was at this hour. A couple of WAVES straggled in from a double date. Shirley exchanged a few words with them.

At last she was off duty. Jim was waiting in the darkened lounge, a street light shining behind him. Shirley entered the lounge, saw him, sitting on a sofa near a window. She joined him there.

They kissed lightly. He brought out a small object from his coat pocket, put it inside her hand, closed her fingers over the object, and said, "Shirley, will you marry me?"

Well, Shirley was not surprised.

"Of course!" she answered.

Then she opened her hand to reveal a small box. She opened it and said, "I can't see. Let's go back on the quarterdeck for a minute."

They walked to the entryway to the quarterdeck. She looked into the box. She gasped at the diamond ring inside.

"My gosh, Jim. Where'd you get this?"

"In London. Do you like it?"

"Like it? I'm crazy about it! Put it on my finger, darling....please! I'm too shaky to do it myself."

He did as she asked. It fit perfectly. As they retreated into the lounge again, he breathed a sigh of relief. *Lucky stiff! What if it hadn't fit? A sign from above. A good sign.*

Before they sat on the sofa again, they put their arms around each other and kissed a long, delectable, and exquisite kiss. Their bodies were in harmony, in sync. They sank onto the sofa together. Each was unable to utter a sound, other than a ragged breathing.

\* \* \*

When they were married in 1950, Shirley was 29, and Jim was 31. She received her discharge from the Navy by reason of marriage within six weeks after they married. Shortly after that, Jim's active reserve duty was ended.

They moved to Seattle where Jim had procured lucrative employment as an airline pilot. They spent two months searching for a house, reasonably close to the airport.

After the required airline company's schooling that included several orientation flights, Jim flew his first commercial flight as first pilot. He was gone for two weeks. At the end of that flight, Shirley made a point of meeting him at the airport.

They hugged. They laughed.

They stood apart, Shirley regarding Jim. She said, "You know,

Hon, you look smashing in a uniform, Navy or airline. You look remarkably splendid, positively elegant!"

"Well," he drawled, and grinned widely, "Thank you, Shirl. You really know how to inflate a man's ego."

"But, we're right back where we started," she said.

"Whaddya mean?"

"You're still flying, and I'm still sweating out the flights, just like in the Navy."

"So it seems. Any complaints?"

"Not really, darling, but I have news."

"Good or bad?"

"Depends. I'm pregnant!"

\* \* \*

Sam was born in 1951; Melinda in 1953; Rachel in 1955; George in 1956; and Mark in late 1957. Their family grew and thrived. Shirley and Jim weathered the "terrible twos" and the "troubled teens." Everyone turned out well, in spite of the difficulties besetting a growing family.

Indeed, Shirley discovered that Sam, the first son, and Melinda, the first daughter, were an enormous help in caring for the little ones that followed.

\* \* \*

The last ten years Jim was associated with the airline, he flew a desk job. He retired in 1984, when he was 65 years old. He was feeling old. Used up. But the grandchildren lit up his life like a beacon. Much to his surprise, the advent of grandchildren made him feel young again, with more pep and vigor than ever before.

Shirley had been his rock. During all the flight schedules through the years, she was at home, caring for the children, looking after the house and yard, and maintaining the cars' safe-driving condition. She never complained. She couldn't, in all good grace; she was too happy for words.

# Chapter Eleven

Helen Enasevich and Rob Erwin sat next to each other at the Esperanza, during the dinner that W/Cdr Michael Reid hosted. Gloria Thomas's memorial service at the chapel was over. Those who had attended went to the restaurant together, along with Sgt. Virgil Blake.

"Helen," Rob said into her ear, "I'm uncomfortable in this rarefied atmosphere."

"Rarefied? What makes this gathering rarefied, Hon?"

"Well, there're two officers here—one of them pretty high-ranking, and from the RAF, for Pete's sake!"

"Rob, Jim Albertson's like a kid brother; and Commander Reid is like an uncle! Nothing rarefied about that."

"Well, you flight attendants are accustomed to being around officers, by the nature of your work. I'm not!"

"Relax, Hon, they won't bite."

He smiled. He reached under the table to squeeze her hand. She squeezed back. And she smiled back.

Bill Wagner, with Angela at his side, saw the surreptitious dive for hands under the table. They were sitting across from Helen and Rob. He smiled inwardly. Then he made his own grope for Angela's hand . . . under the table.

Back at the base, Bill dropped off the four back-seat passengers at the WAVES Barracks. Everyone said good night to each other.

Rob took Helen to the bottom step of the WAVES barracks, put his arms around her, and said, "That was a nice service for Gloria. It was *very* nice of Commander Reid to take all of us to dinner. It was a nice dinner. . . Can't I say anything other than 'nice'?"

"No, and it doesn't matter. So give me a *nice* kiss!"

When they finished, and she drew back a bit, she went on to say, "But then, my dear, *all* your kisses are nice."

"That's because you're so nice to kiss!"

"Don't change, Rob. Don't ever change. I love you exactly as you are!"

"Sweets, I love you, too. More than you can ever know."

"Oh, I think I know."

They kissed again, and she disentangled herself from his arms and ran up the steps. At the top step, she turned, said "Good night," and blew him another kiss. He returned it.

\* \* \*

In 1950 Rob Erwin made 1st class aviation mech. He asked Helen to marry him. She wanted to accept as graciously as she could manage, but first, she had to tell him something that could come between them. She had anticipated this moment with Rob, and she had prepared what she would say to him.

They sat on a couch at the USO, just outside the base. With trepidation, she began.

"Rob, there's something you need to know about me, and we need to discuss it at length. Get it all out in the open."

"What're you getting at, Helen?"

"You remember our squadron's plane crash in the desert awhile back?"

"Remember it! It was the talk of the squadron—for weeks! Why, what about it?"

"I was the sole survivor."

"That was *you*? Holy Mackerel! I had no idea! Oh, Honey, what an awful experience that must've been!"

"Well, it *was* awful. At first. Then I met Sheik Abdul Goshen, chief of his tribe, Emir of his emirate."

"Huh! That's a mouthful."

"Darling, I'll try to be brief, but I hope what I'm going to tell you will not be upsetting."

His brow furrowed. He said, "Go on."

"The whole time I was in the Arab encampment, at an oasis, I was treated fairly and fed and housed, albeit in a tent!"

He smiled. She continued. "Abdul and I had a romance. He wanted me to marry him, but I refused. For pity's sake, I would've been his fourth wife! And . . . I couldn't bring myself to marry a Muslim, with or without three other wives."

"So what happened then?" he said, becoming serious again.

"So, on the last day of traveling from the oasis, just before I was met by the Navy Liaison Officer to go to the airfield, Abdul gave me this ring as a memento of my visit to the desert." She was wearing it, as usual, and placed her hand on top of his, for him to see it.

"I've already noticed the ring and often wondered about it. Wondered where in the world did you get a ring like that! It's quite . . . dazzling . . ."

"Rob, darling, I'll never wear it again, if you find it to be too much, too ostentatious."

"Oh, Honey, I couldn't ask you to do that. It's too beautiful to put away in a box for the rest of your life. No, you keep the ring and wear it . . . all the time, if you wish."

"It doesn't make you feel threatened? Intimidated?"

"Heck, no, Helen. You're here with me, and the sheik is how many thousands of miles away? Sweating in a desert? With his three wives? Naw, I'm not threatened by your wearing his ring. It's too gorgeous to hide."

"Oh, Rob, what a sweetheart you are. And utterly, completely understanding!"

Cautiously, he said, "Of course, you're reminded of the guy every time you look at the ring."

Yes, of course. But, Rob, that doesn't keep me from giving you my complete loyalty."

A pause. He asked, "You still love him, Helen?"

"I was strongly attracted to him, Rob, right from the beginning. I would be lying if I said otherwise. And, yes, I did love him—but not as a fiancé, not as a future mate. Not that. I think I was in love with the experience. I felt . . . swept up by the moment, by the sheer glamour of it all—a wealthy emir, all that grandeur in his palace, even in his tent at the oasis there was an abundance of luxury. It was impressive!"

He looked down at his interlaced hands.

She went on. "But that kind of life just isn't for me, Rob. I'd have never fit in with all that exotic indulgence. Not in a million years."

Then he looked into her eyes, wanting desperately to believe what she was saying to him.

"Dearest Rob," she said, "I give you my undying love. I mean that from the bottom of my heart."

"So, your answer to my proposal is 'yes'?"

"Oh, *yes*, Darling. And no one nor anything can change my mind! I'm locked in. You can count on that."

"So," he said, smiling again, "as they say in the movies, let's close the deal with a kiss."

"I thought we'd never get around to it!"

\* \* \*

In 1951, just before the end of Helen's enlistment, they were married in the chapel at Pax River. They chose that time because Helen wanted to be married in uniform. That was more important to her than a big, splashy wedding with a long, white wedding gown, and all the trimmings.

Frugality was behind it all because Rob's enlistment was also ending soon, and he was in a dither about what to do: re-enlist? or face the cruel world outside? Whatever he did, both he and Helen were determined to put college in their lives. No matter what it took to manage it. All he had to do was make the big decision—to stay in or to get out.

Frugality became their byword.

Helen, in a letter to Shirley Jackson Albertson, told her of Rob's indecision. Shirley read the letter to Jim that same morning she received it, while Jim was between flights.

Upon finishing the letter, Jim said, "D'you remember the phone number for the squadron, Honey?"

"Sure."

He picked up the phone and said, "Okay, how does it go?"

She related it to him. When the CO's yeoman answered, Jim asked to be connected to the hangar flight office.

He then asked, "May I speak to Petty Officer Erwin? Rob Erwin?"

"Just a sec."

"Hello?"

"Rob?"

"Yes."

"Jim Albertson. Remember me?"

"Of course, sir."

"Forget the 'sir' stuff, Rob. I'm not in the military anymore. I hear you're having doubts about what to do at the end of your enlistment."

"Well, yessir, I am. But how would you know that?"

"Helen wrote to Shirley. She just read the letter to me."

"And?"

"And, I'm telling you, Rob, take the discharge and come immediately out here to Seattle. My airlines company is *begging* for aviation mechanics!"

"No kidding?"

"Just do it! Get out here as fast as you can! You can stay with us. The boys have an extra bunk bed. That won't be a problem for you, will it?"

"Nossir. Not after living in a Navy barracks!"

"Sure." A chuckle. Then, "When's your enlistment up?"

"Next month, the 16th."

"I'll see you no later than the 17th. Call me to tell me when your flight arrives. If I'm on a flight myself, Shirley and the kids'll pick you up. I'll have everything arranged for an interview the next day, after your arrival. Don't let me down, Rob!"

By now, Rob's enthusiasm had risen. "Oh, I won't, sir. Believe me!"

* * *

The interview was successful. Rob was hired on the spot. He and

Helen moved into an apartment. Helen got a job at the same airline company as Rob, in an office. Their hours were the same.

They both signed up for evening classes at a local college.

"Thank goodness for VA benefits!" Helen exclaimed.

"You got that right, honey. With my new job's good pay, we'll have enough saved up very soon for a house. Let's go house-hunting this weekend!"

Caught up in the headiness of all that was happening, Helen made some mental calculations and realized that if they could live on her paycheck, they could save Rob's entire pay, and they'd indeed have a down payment in a short time.

"Yes! Let's!" Helen was enthralled. "I want to live near the Albertsons. How do you feel about that, Hon?"

"Sweetheart, I'm all for it! If it weren't for your letter to Shirley and then Jim's phone call to me, there's no telling what we'd be doing now! I owe Jim big time. . . I owe you, Honey."

\* \* \*

In June 1958, Rob and Helen graduated from college. Night classes took more than four years to get a degree. On graduation day, Helen was already five months pregnant with their first child.

Six weeks after graduation, Rob came home from work, grubby, sweaty, and tired. He said to Helen, "I'm no longer a grease monkey!"

"What're you talking about, Honey?" she asked guardedly.

"Beginning next week, I start work as a mechanical engineer, for the airlines!"

"Rob! Congratulations! It came through! I knew it would!"

"It's all your doing, Helen. You're the one who encouraged me to apply for the job, to get ready for the umpteen interviews, to dress for them, and so on."

"But YOU got the job!"

"YES!" He grinned widely. "We need to go shopping this week. I need some new suits!"

"Of course!" she exclaimed, happily.

\* \* \*

Kay Erwin was born in October of 1958; her mother, Helen, was 37. When Kay was two weeks old, a package arrived at the house, addressed to the new baby.

Helen, opening the package, was mystified. It contained 100 gold Krugerand coins. There was no letter, no note. A princely sum to be spent for a new baby. She looked at the postmark: Rabat, Morocco.

*Rabat Morocco? This couldn't be from anyone else but Abdul! I'm stunned! How on earth did he find me? How did he know I was married? How did he know I had a baby girl?*

She had to show the gift to Rob. What in the world would his reaction be? She worried about it all day. When Rob came home from his airlines office, she was still in a lather about how to show him the gift. Finally, she blurted it out.

"Rob, Honey, a package came today from Morocco for the baby: 100 Krugerands. Here." She handed him the package.

"Krugerands? A hundred of them? What's that all about?" Immediately, it dawned on him. "The sheik, right?"

"Must be. No card, no note, no communication of any kind. Just the package. I don't know what to make of it. I have no idea how he knows where I am, that I'm married, that I have a new baby daughter . . ."

"So, you've never been in touch with him, Helen?"

"Of course not! I swear it!"

"I believe you, Honey. But it is a mystery. There has to be an explanation. However, I'm sure it's from the sheik, too. Very generous of him!"

"I'm at a loss for words."

"It's okay, Honey. We can handle it. Together."

"Darling, I love you so much, sometimes it hurts!"

"Oh, I know the feeling, Sweetheart. I know it, too."

\* \* \*

Greg was born in 1959 and Paul in 1960.

"Oo-ee," said Helen in the hospital with their last baby, Paul. "I'm pushing 40 and still having babies."

"Well, Honey," Rob replied, "three was our limit, and we've arrived. Now you can relax. . . What am I saying? Relax? With two toddlers and an infant? I must be out of my gourd!"

"We'll manage, Hon. Really, we will."

\* \* \*

The Erwins and the Albertsons had become best friends—good and loyal friends. They picnicked together every summer. One year they all piled into their two station wagons and camped out for a week. In later years, they took a cruise together—their entire families. They enjoyed it so much that two years afterwards, they did it again, different destination.

Mark Albertson was 10 months older than Kay Erwin, but since his birthday was in December, and hers was the following October, they ended up in the same kindergarten class. He was too young to start school, not turning 5 until December, three months after the start of the school year; and she was just barely eligible, by turning 5 one month after the same school year began. Therefore, they were in the same classes throughout the elementary, junior high, and high school years.

When Kay Erwin was in fifth grade, she came home at the end of a school day and said to her mother, "Mom, there's a boy at school who likes me."

"How do you know that, Honey?"

"He trips me in the hallway and shoves me on the playground!"

"I see. And what's the boy's name?"

Kay blushed. "It's Mark Albertson."

\* \* \*

Kay Erwin and Mark Albertson were highschool sweethearts. They dated all through college. As early as the first year of college, it was agreed between them that they would marry as soon as Mark began his first job, after graduation. The first week after graduation, he was hired as an aeronautical engineer at Boeing.

After the first month of his employment, and after their wedding and weekend honeymoon, Kay asked him, "So, Honey, how's the new job going? Can you handle it okay?"

"Oh, yes! It's a snap . . . and a pleasure!"

"But Mark, I know we've talked about this before. Your dad wanted you to be a pilot, didn't he?"

"He surely did! Especially since Sam turned out to be a commercial artist, and George has opened his own health-food store."

"How's the store coming along, Honey?"

"Quite well, from all reports. Before he even opened the store, he hired a bio-chemist/nutritionist to counsel him on what products to put onto the shelves. Her name's Sylvia . . . she's attractive and has gray hair."

"Is she still at the store?"

"Yes. She got the inventory pretty well set up when she asked George if she could stay on as a part-time clerk or cashier. She wanted to be able to set up a nutrition class now and then. They have the space at the back of the store."

"So, did he do that?"

"Oh, yeah. They're going to be married next year."

"They are! Next year? Why so long an engagement?"

"She has to wait for her divorce to become final."

"Oh." She continued with, "Isn't Sylvia a bit old for George?" She regretted the question as soon as she asked it.

"Maybe not. She may be gray-haired, but she's prematurely gray. True, she's older than George, but not that much. He really depends on her for helping him run the store. He can do the business part, but he needs the nutritionist to keep the products current."

"Sounds like a nice arrangement—for both of them."

"It is."

She said, "And now, both your brothers are successful. And, for that matter, so are your sisters. Melinda, the nurse, married her boss, the doctor. And Rachel is married to her job as an accountant, while she studies for CPA."

"She's going to make it, too. I'd bet my entire estate—such as it is—on that." Mark was thoughtful for a moment, then continued, "I know I didn't follow in my dad's footsteps, as he wished me to do, by being a pilot. But what the heck. I design the stuff they fly!"

"Close enough!" she said.

\* \* \*

Greg and Paul Erwin, in 1978, enlisted in the Marine Corps. They each served one four-year hitch. After discharge, they both entered college in San Diego on the GI Bill. Both of them were a few years older than the other freshmen, and their classmates called them "the old men."

And that was okay with them. It gave them a feeling of superiority—in experience, if not in proficiency . . . yet.

They double-dated a pair of twin sisters all through college. After graduation, they married the twins. The two young men signed up for Police Academy in San Diego and eventually were assigned to that police force.

Their children were double cousins to each other.

\* \* \*

Rob retired from the airlines at age 65 in 1990. He and Helen began traveling extensively by both air and cruising. It became a main preoccupation that turned into a passion. Of course, having free airlines passes helped.

Between travels, they got re-acquainted with the growing number of grandchildren, bringing them gifts from ports around the world.

Rob and Helen were as devoted to each other as they were in their first years together. They both were, eventually, white-haired. They both stayed slim. They were an attractive couple to present to the world.

And everyone they met admired them and liked them instantly.

"Life is beautiful," they often said to each other.

# Chapter 12

While the other guests sipped coffee and after-dinner drinks, Bill and Angela held hands, under the table, at the Esperanza Restaurant. After Michael paid the check, everyone departed in the two cars in which they had arrived.

At the WAVES Barracks, Bill's four back-seat passengers alighted. Everyone said good night to each other. Bill kissed Angela. She started to open the passenger-side door.

"Hon-ney," Bill said, "can't you stay a little longer?"

"Sorry, dear. I have to get to bed early—for tomorrow's flight."

"Of course! I'd hoped you'd forgotten about that." He left his driver's seat, went around the Packard, and gently pulled her out of that side of the car.

She looked at him wistfully. "Wish I'd forgotten about it, too . . . Goodnight, sweetheart." She kissed him again.

"Goodnight, darlin'. Have a safe trip," he said, holding her a little longer while he gave her a kiss back. "I'll think about you every moment you're gone, Angela."

"Thanks, Bill. I'll think about you, too, constantly."

She went up the steps quickly. She turned and waved to him. He waved back. Then she was gone.

\* \* \*

Bill drove back to his barracks, Rob Erwin accompanying him. On the way, while making small talk with Rob, he thought about Angela . . . and him. About both of them, together. *Well, I'm having some serious thoughts about that girl. Been dating her for about a year now. Hmm, most I've ever dated anyone. Well, that doesn't necessarily mean anything.*

They entered the barracks, they took their showers, and they headed for their respective bunks. Flopping down onto his lower bunk, Bill thought about Angela, and about his life.

He was born in 1922 in Salt Lake City, Utah (he was not a Mormon). He had worked in the print room of a Salt Lake City newspaper. He had been an amateur radio operator since high school, where he built his first radio set.

*I'd like to build another rig and start hamming again, but there's no place here where I can set it up. Have to wait until I get transferred someplace where I can live ashore. Then I could set up the gear.*

Interrupting his ham radio hobby in 1942, he took a battery of Navy tests involving radar. His composite grade was so high that he received a rating of 2nd class radioman upon his enlistment in the

Navy. It was an accomplishment to be proud of.

*Not bad, if I do say so, myself! Everyone else starts out as an apprentice seaman and works up to 3rd class, then 2nd class. I have a leg up on a lot of guys!*

Upon finishing three stages of radar schools, he spent two weeks in a teachers' class in Chicago. Then he was transferred to a Naval Reserve unit in Michigan City, Indiana, to teach what he had learned in the first three schools he had attended. His abilities were recognized by the right people, and they were put to work.

*Boy, was I a lucky stiff to get stateside duty while the war raged around the world! What the devil will I tell my grandchildren when they ask me, 'Grandpa, what did you do in the war?'*

The war came to an end in August 1945. A few months later, he was transferred to VR-3 at Pax. He was a radio operator on squadron flights, both domestic and, later on, abroad. He loved the flights abroad.

*Gives me a chance to see the world! The world I didn't get to see during the war. But who's complaining? Not me! Besides, I'd never have met Angela without this duty. That has to count for something. I really like her, better'n all the other girls I've dated. And I've had my share! No question about that.*

*Angela, Angela, will I dream about you again tonight? Come to me, Angela, my sweet, in my dreams . . .*

He fell asleep.

* * *

Later the next week, Angela said to him, while they walked together from the movie and back to her barracks, "Bill, you and I have been dating for about a year, haven't we?"

"Yep." He wondered what she was leading up to.

She waited before continuing. Their walking slowed.

She said, "Tomorrow's Saturday. You have the duty then?"

"No. Why?"

"I have a flight on Sunday. Can you and I go to Solomons Island tomorrow? I want to talk to you."

"Well, sure, Honey. But why can't we talk here and now? Or in your barracks lounge? Tonight?"

"Well," she replied, "I want us to be away from Navy and people we know. As far as possible."

"Why? What're you getting at?"

"No more talk about it just now. Can we take a noon boat to Solomons tomorrow? Lunch at the restaurant, my treat."

"How can a guy turn down an offer like that!"

\* \* \*

They finished eating lunch and were having coffee.

Bill said, "Okay. What's this all about?"

Angela looked at him, then down at her coffee. She looked up at him again. She began. "Bill, there's something I want to tell you about. Maybe you've already heard rumors. Maybe not."

He frowned and said, "Honey, I have no idea what you're referring to!"

"I know. I'm getting off to a bad start." She tried once more. "There's something I want to tell you. On one of my flights last year—a flight to Bermuda—I met someone who was important to me, briefly. Very briefly. Part of an afternoon and an evening."

She paused, wondering where to go next in the story.

He said, "So?"

"So. Seems he is a duke, from England. Kurt Beckwaithe."

"So?" he asked again.

"After tea that day at his house on a beach in Bermuda, and after dinner, I returned to Hamilton Air Force Base. Next morning, the flight returned to Pax. I never saw him again."

He looked puzzled. "And?"

She took a deep breath. "After my next flight, to Iceland, I returned to the barracks where there was a letter waiting for me, from him. He had returned to England and wrote the letter from there."

A nod of the head by Bill. Another deep breath by Angela. "He wrote that he loved me and wished he could ask me to marry him, but he couldn't. His mother's requirements were that his wife be titled, and I gathered his mother also wanted his wife to be wealthy."

"So, what'd you do?"

"Nothing. Except . . . he had sent along with the letter a gold chain with a pendant on it. The pendant was his family crest. He asked that I accept it and think of him each time I wore it."

"Well!" Bill was beginning to wonder what all this had to do with him. It put him on edge. And on guard. He thought, *What the hell is she telling this to me for?* He decided to ask that question, openly. "Why, my dear Angela, are you telling me this?"

"Well, I'm not sure. We've been so close this past year, you and I. Whatever happens, I wanted you to know about Kurt Beckwaithe. What he meant to me for such a short while. But the feelings I had for him are . . . largely missing, beginning with the time I met you that night on a flight."

"Beckwaithe? That the duke's name?"

"Yes."

"You ever wear the pendant?"

"All the time."

"So, you think of him all the time."

"Not really." She looked him in the eye. "I think about you most of the time. Just about all the time. I care for you a lot, Bill. Did you know that?"

"I kinda figured it. And I had hoped you cared for me. Because I care for you!" *Whoa, Buddy. Getting into dangerous territory here. I never told a girl before that I CARED FOR HER!*

She smiled grandly at him. He got over his feeling scared.

She said, "Anytime you want me to take off the chain and pendant, just say the word, and I'll do it."

"Naw, Angie, you don't have to do that. But let me see it."

She pulled the pendant out through the neckline of her uniform and showed it to him. He reached across the table, cradling the pendant against two fingers.

"Family crest, you said? What's it mean?"

"I don't know the symbolism of it. It's just a family crest. Like a logo. I don't know."

He dropped the crest back onto her uniform tie. "And you say you don't think of him all the time?"

"That's what I said, and that's as true as it can be. I think of you, Bill, all the time."

"Wear it as much as you like, Angie. It's okay with me. And thanks for offering to remove it."

She began to breathe easily once more.

Angela paid the check, and they took a walk through the village until time to catch the next boat back to the base. On the 35-minute boat ride, they held hands, tightly.

Angela felt relieved. She felt freed. She was especially pleased that Bill did not seem to be troubled by her wearing the crest.

The boat's engine noise was too great to be able to talk. They rode in silence, each with his and her thoughts.

"Honey," he said, as they stepped onto the dock at the base, "what would you like to do next?"

"What do you suggest?"

"You know," he said, as they approached his Packard, "we've never ridden around the whole base. It's a big base, for sure. Let's take a ride around it and see what's what!"

"I'm for that!"

For evening chow, each had to go to his own chow hall. Bill called her at her barracks afterward. "Can I come over to kiss you good night, Honey?"

"Can't think of a better way to end a perfect day!"

* * *

Bill lay on his lower bunk in his barracks that night, totally wired. He couldn't figure out why he couldn't sleep. His mind was going in circles: *Can't figure out why Angie felt she had to tell me about the duke. She told me she cared for me. I told her I cared for her. A BIG step for me, by George!*

*So, if she cares for me, and I care for her, what next? I know what next. Marriage! Marriage? Must be nuts! I've never considered marriage with any girl I've known.*

*How did the word 'marriage' come into the picture? I don't remember thinking about it before.*

He tried to put this line of thinking out of his head. He wished he could see Angela again, before she left on her flight tomorrow.

*Good Lord! Tomorrow is already here!*

* * *

Angela's flight from the Azores was to Germany. On the return leg from the Azores back to St. John's, Newfoundland, her plane's number three engine began throwing oil. The engine was cut. Then the number four engine began throwing oil as well. Both engines on the starboard side were now non-functioning. As the plane lost altitude, the plane commander cut the two starboard engines on again, but only long enough to gain the lost altitude.

Meanwhile, to lighten the aircraft's weight, the plane commander ordered all luggage to be jettisoned from the cargo hold, as well as every piece of loose gear in the cockpit and main cabin with the following exceptions: the water urn, and the navigation kit, along with the navigator's pens and pencils. The plane commander couldn't get rid of the check-off list for landing, however, not only because it was necessary to make a landing safely but because it was chained to the cockpit bulkhead.

Crew and passengers were allowed to keep their IDs and paper money, but not coins. *Everything else had to go!*

Weather set in at St. John's. The plane was diverted to Sydney, Nova Scotia. Headwinds picked up. Fuel was getting low. Making it to Sydney was an iffy situation.

All that information was tracked by Bill, who dogged the Operations (Ops) Office. He made a nuisance of himself, trying to learn the latest developments for Angela's flight. He was worried sick.

One of the clerks in Ops said to Bill, "What gives with you,

Wagner? You've been following that crippled plane for hours!"

"Special cargo on board, Man."

"What the hell does that mean?"

Bill replied, "My girl. My best girl. I'm worried out of my mind about her!"

"Oh." Rolling his eyes, the clerk turned away.

Bill prayed for the plane, the crew, and for Angie. It was awkward. He hadn't prayed since he was a small child. It all came back to him—how to pray.

Then he prayed some more.

At last, a teletype message reported the aircraft's safe landing at Sydney. Crew and passengers were bussed from the airport into town and were quartered in various small hotels and room-and-board houses. Toiletries and fresh underwear and white shirts were supplied by merchants in the city, gratis. Once more, U.S.-Canadian relations were cemented.

Bill immediately went to Ops and asked if a substitute plane were going to be sent to Sydney to pick up the stranded crew and passengers. It was. He went to the scheduling Chief. He volunteered to go as radioman on that flight. The Chief put him on it.

The plane from Pax left four hours later. Bill tried to get some sleep before the flight, but he was too keyed up. All he wanted was to see Angie and put his arms around her and . . .

* * *

When Bill's aircraft arrived at Sydney, and got refueled, the stranded crew and passengers soon showed up in busses at the hangar at the airport.

Bill strained to see the people coming off the busses. At last he spotted Angela. He ran to her as fast as he could go. She saw him coming toward her. And she ran toward him.

They embraced upon impact.

"Angie, Hon-ney! I was so worried about you! You all right?"

"Yes, Bill. What in the world are you doing here?"

He told her about his arranging to come as a crewman with the relief plane. He wouldn't let her go, he was so happy to see that she was okay. She didn't mind.

"Angie! Darling!" he said while still clinging to her. "Will you marry me?"

She began to laugh. She pushed away from him, saying, "It took an emergency to bring you to ask me THAT?"

"It sure did. Made me see the light. I was so afraid for you, afraid I'd lost you! So, how 'bout it, Honey? You wanna get married?"

"Of course! Let's do it!" she replied, laughing and crying, at the same time.

* * *

Angie and her fellow deadheading crew members, and the passengers, continued their interrupted flight schedule to Westover, deecee, and to Pax in the relief plane. Bill, still a member of the relief plane, was busy, as the only radioman in his crew. But the deadheading radiomen spelled him at various times during the remainder of the flight.

When they returned at last to Pax, Bill and Angie turned in their paper work at the terminal; they sought out each other. They embraced once more. They both laughed and cried, again. They were so relieved that the ordeal was over. They were so happy.

* * *

Shortly after the crippled-flight episode, Bill was sent to a school for aviation electronics. He graduated second in his class and received his changed 1st class rate from radioman to aviation electronics technician.

Angie continued flying while Bill was away at school. Their long-distance telephone costs were horrendous.

Bill said, "I don't care if I go broke calling you, Honey. I've got to be in touch with you every night!"

"I'll go broke with you, Sweetheart," Angela responded. Anytime!"

"Darlin', you're a real sweetheart! Good night, Dear."

"Good night, Honey."

* * *

When Bill finished his schooling and received his new rate, it was time for him and Angela to make serious plans.

They were married in 1950. She was 26, and he was 30. Angela stayed on in the Navy, according to plan, as long as they could be stationed together.

Their Navy housing at Patuxent was on an otherwise closed Navy base one-half mile north of Solomons Island. The island had special significance for them. They had had the discussion about Kurt Beckwaithe there, and they had weathered that storm gracefully.

They were delighted to get housing anywhere, in spite of the inconvenience: The boat schedules became a vital part of their lives.

There were fun times, between flights, and on an occasional weekend. They borrowed a Navy neighbor's inflated rubber life raft and went oaring up Old Mill Creek (an inlet between the peninsula and the Chesapeake Bay). They picnicked on narrow, white, hard-packed sand beaches. They bought a canoe. They paddled onto a beach overgrown with brush and an ancient black-walnut tree, collected the black walnuts into the canoe and returned to their half-Quonset-hut quarters. After shelling the black walnuts, their hands were badly stained, for months. It was worth it. Boxes of the nuts had been shipped out to various relatives, who enjoyed them thoroughly.

They paddled, one Saturday, into a quiet cove, both leaning over the gunwale and looking at the marine life beneath them. A presence, felt by both, prompted them to look up and behind them. There, a few yards away, standing in a boat with an outboard motor, was a man in a khaki uniform (no insignia) and dark glasses, hands on hips, weapon suspended from his belt.

He waved to them and said, "Just checking for oyster poachers. Continue with what you're doing." Then he was gone.

"What on earth?" they asked each other.

*  *  *

In 1951, the squadron was moved to NAS Corpus Christi, Texas, and Bill made Chief.

They had barely settled in their Navy housing at Corpus when Angela learned that she was pregnant. She applied for honorable discharge from the Navy by reason of pregnancy. Six weeks later, the discharge took place.

Angela had mixed feelings. She really liked the Navy and felt a bittersweet longing for that part of her life, which was now and forever over. A few days of nostalgia and near-depression overtook her. But remembering that she had to prepare for her baby's birth, down the line, brought her back to reality.

The reality she faced was that, through Bill, she would be connected to the Navy as a Navy wife until he retired. He had previously declared himself a 30-year man. And that was very much okay with Angela.

Her news of the pregnancy had been cause for celebration. Afterward, another kind of news reached Angela.

It was in a magazine from England that arrived in the mail, addressed to her. *Who in the world is sending me a magazine, out of the blue, from England? And why?*

She perused the magazine. And then she spotted the reason it was sent to her. It had a full-spread, color-photo article about the lavish wedding of Kurt Beckwaithe, the Duke of Branbury, and his bride, a dark-haired, dark-eyed beauty from Spain. She was the daughter of a successful and outrageously wealthy Spanish industrialist.

The spread took her breath away! She pored over the article and photos. She noticed something vaguely familiar. Of course, Kurt, now 47 (according to the article), was a familiar face. But, there was something more.

Then it dawned on her. The bride looked strikingly like Angela!

The dark hair, dark eyes. Even the bride's features were very much like Angela's.

She smiled a private smile. She knew. She knew Kurt had chosen someone who resembled Angela herself. And, even though the bride was not royalty, Kurt had found a woman who was moneyed. Apparently Kurt's mother was satisfied about *that*!

*Well,* she thought, *I certainly wish the happy couple—and they do look happy—a successful marriage. Good for you, Kurt! You found the opportunity, and you really went for it!*

*Although I still wear his crest, and I have thought about him, in the fringes of my mind, I can rest easily. . . he found a mate! Again, Kurt, good for you!*

Another thought invaded her head: *How on earth did Kurt know where to send the magazine? How did he know my married name, my address? Seemingly everything about me! I wonder?*

When Bill returned to their quarters at dinnertime, Angela showed him the magazine.

"This is the Duke?" he asked.

"The one and the same."

"Kinda old, isn't he?" To himself, he breathed a sigh of relief.

"I suppose so," she replied, wanting to add, 'but distinguished.' However, she did not.

Bill was still appraising the Duke: "But very stately looking, I'd say."

"True."

"So, you fell for an old guy, Angie?"

"Well, that was about four years ago. He was four years younger."

Bill did the simple math. "He must've been about 43?"

"Probably."

"He was still an old guy, even then."

"I guess so."

He viewed the photos once more, saying, "She looks like you. He must've been thinking about you all along."

"Maybe."

He said, "I know I would, if I had to give you up—like he did. I'd think about you the rest of my life."

She had no response but waited.

He put down the magazine, dismissing it. "Dinner ready, Hon?"

"Sure is." Inexplicably and silently, she emitted a long a sigh. She felt as though a heavy load had been lifted from her shoulders.

* * *

Janet was born in 1952, while the family was still in Texas. By 1953, they were transferred to Rio de Janeiro, Brazil. Bill was assigned to be the radioman on the Admiral's aircraft, an R4D: two engines, a galley, 18 passengers, four crew members.

It was a vastly interesting and satisfying duty for all three of the Wagners. Janet learned to speak Portuguese as a toddler, talking with the maid, playing with the Brazilian neighborhood children, and even able, when necessary, to transact purchases and other business for Angela, when her Portuguese language knowledge failed her.

Bill was gone on flights approximately two-thirds of the time. Angela learned to travel throughout the city by bus routes, taking Janet along with her on each outing.

Eventually they ordered an automobile from the States, and now Angela and Janet were freer to explore the city, shop at the local feirias (street markets), and visit their American, Canadian, and British friends. Angela reached out to her Brazilian neighbors and gained a few lasting friendships among them.

In 1955 they returned to the States for a 10-month course for Bill at the Naval Technical Training Center, Memphis, Tennessee. Actually, the Center was in a small town near Memphis, called Millington. His course was for advanced aviation electronics. His ability was now two-fold: radio operation and electronics maintenance and repair.

After the electronics course, in late 1955, they were transferred to Guam and were assigned quarters on the Naval Air Station. David was born in 1956.

During the Guam experience, they had two R and Rs (Rest and Recreation): one to Tokyo; and one to Hong Kong.

From Guam they were transferred in 1958 to NAS Point Mugu, California. Then, they found themselves back at Pax from 1960 to 1963.

At the beginning of 1960, Bill took the test first for E-8 (Senior Chief), and made it. The next year, he took the test for E-9 (Master Chief) and made that as well. Celebrations for the promotions were gratifying. E-9 was as high as any enlisted man could go. Angela was so proud of him!

During the Pax duty, Bill was sent on a five-month deployment with his squadron to the Mediterranean, aboard an aircraft carrier. Each time the ship put into port, Bill secured a few days leave and visited the area extensively. He shopped avidly: an accordion from Italy (which he shipped back to Angela at Pax); a gold bracelet from Athens; a gold pendant from Jerusalem, etched with an Arab symbol, to be attached to the bracelet; an alexandrite ring from Beirut; and a wool cape from Istanbul. Angela was delighted with all of it.

Near the end of 1963, Bill was 47 years old and had put in his 30 years. It was time to retire. Forty-seven was too young to just quit working—quit living. They moved into a house outside the base. It was the first house they ever owned.

He found employment with a contractor on the base at Pax. He was an electronics consultant to electronics engineers, who needed, from time-to-time, advice on how their designs actually performed in the field. He enjoyed his job to the max, doing an extensively satisfying work.

* * *

Janet and David both enlisted in the Navy, right out of high school. They both had served in the JNROTC (Junior Naval Reserve Officer Training Corps). They both had loved the Navy life, with their parents, bending with the wind of changes experienced at each transfer.

Janet married a naval officer, Brett, and, with the updated Navy policy for married couples, they were always transferred together. Also, women in the Navy were not forced to leave the service with each pregnancy and childbirth. Janet and Brett had successful careers, living a more-than-satisfying life. They had two children.

David, following exactly in his father's footsteps, became an avionics technician (new Navy name for aviation electronics). He met a young woman in the Navy, Ronnie (for Veronica), during his first duty station after the training course. She was a yeoman in the same squadron. And, like Janet and her husband, they married and were able to stay together in the Navy. They had three children, and they thrived on their shared lives.

* * *

Angela was happy to be back at where it all started between her and Bill. She dug in for the long haul of completing their lives and for whatever was in store for them.

What was in store for them was the opportunity to travel space-available on MAC aircraft. They could visit their children and become acquainted with each new grandchild with little effort on their part.

With Bill's job, and with their traveling opportunities, they enjoyed the "golden" years.

Angela died in 1985, at age 61, of breast cancer.

# Chapter Thirteen

Elizabeth Holmes continued her free-wheeling lifestyle. How could her popularity remain over the years? To answer that, one must consider her continued blonde-to-white-hairedness, her continued petite figure, and her continued outgoing personality.

The fact was: Men were attracted to her. All men. All her life.

Elizabeth was the only one of the flight attendants at the end of the 1940s to remain in the Navy for a 20-year hitch. Upon her retirement, she moved to Washington, D.C. and went to work at the Pentagon as a civil servant.

Her assignment was the Navy Protocol Office.

The Pentagon! So many men to choose from (and in Elizabeth's case, the men did the choosing). She thought she'd died and gone to heaven. Even when the military men at the Pentagon were transferred elsewhere, their replacements came on board, and she could start all over.

"I swear!" exclaimed one of Elizabeth's office co-workers. "That woman is something else!"

"What woman?" asked a second co-worker.

"Elizabeth Holmes, of course!"

"What do you mean?" asked Co-worker Number Two.

"You know what I mean. The way Elizabeth Holmes dates every pair of pants that comes into this office! And they're all officers, exclusively. Don't tell me you haven't noticed?"

"Oh, that. Sure, I've noticed," said Co-worker Number Two. "It is a bit amazing, isn't it?"

"You kidding me? I think it's scandalous!" Co-worker Number One was beside herself over the subject.

"You're just jealous!"

"You taking her side?" asked Co-worker Number One, with disgust.

"No. . . " said Co-worker Number Two. She made a face. "I'm jealous, too . . ."

\* \* \*

Four years before her second retirement, and this one was from federal civil service, she met one man at the Pentagon who literally swept her off her feet. Elizabeth suffered a setback, so it seemed to her, later on, by marrying him.

He was a fast-talking four-flusher who could talk himself into and out of any situation that came along. He was Commander Richard A. Whitson, a retired naval officer. He was always doing some administration work in the naval service. He had served his 30 years in stateside duty with two exceptions: He served three years in Hawaii; and he served a six-month temporary duty assignment in Ottawa, Canada. He was never aboard a naval vessel, even as a visitor, in his life.

Commader Whitson, upon retirement from the Navy, was more of a PR man, flaunting his charm and silver-tongued speech right and left.

The flamboyant commander actually talked Elizabeth Holmes, veteran bachelor woman, into marrying him. He had courted her grandly and led her into the deep and sometimes murky waters of matrimony.

Elizabeth got her feet back onto solid ground, soon enough, when the smooth talk drove her to distraction and . . . into sheer boredom. She often wondered, *Whatever in the world happened to my senses? My brain?*

In less than a year, they were divorced.

\* \* \*

At the end of her second retirement, she moved back to her original home, San Francisco.

"Mother," she said to her, now in her eighties, "Have you noticed how many homosexuals there seem to be in the city these days?"

"Notice it? I've seen it, heard it, and breathed it for a couple of decades now."

"They're all over the place!" exclaimed Elizabeth.

"So it seems."

"A gay-pride parade coming up this week."

"Every year—like clockwork."

Elizabeth mulled this over. She put two and two together and came up with a monumental answer/decision. *This city isn't for me! Time to move on . . . where the pastures are greener.*

So, Elizabeth moved to Salt Lake City. Bad choice again. So many women, so few men.

Elizabeth moved once more, this time to New York City. With the huge population, there were more men to choose from . . . or more men to choose her. Aging was never a problem with Elizabeth. She was still alluring, white hair, smile wrinkles and all.

The chore of finding a job was not difficult. She secured part-time employment with an investment company. Her thoughts on that revealed the lifetime longing for male companionship, on *her* terms. *I have to work part time, at least. How else am I going to meet attractive and interesting men? Ah, here comes that new vice-president of the company. He's so-o-o dreamy! Recently divorced, I hear.*

\* \* \*

Elizabeth never again wanted to settle down with one man, in a marriage. And why should she? She had so much fun, unattached. The one disastrous marriage convinced her she was not meant to be shackled to someone else. She had no wifely duties and loyalties to maintain; she had no children to raise and nurture. Nesting was never her ultimate goal.

It was her individual choice to remain single, after that one attempt at wedlock. No one, not even the most dedicated romantic, could fault her for that. She was as happy as a clam.

\* \* \*

Elizabeth Holmes did, at last, and at least, take on a roommate: a large, aggressive male cat.

# EPILOGUE

In 1981, some NATS/MATS VR personnel established annual reunions. The former flight attendants and their spouses were among those who participated in these reunions.

Jean Trimwood Reid managed to make her annual trek back to America during reunion time. Every other year, Michael accompanied her.

Gradually, the following occurred: first, one participating member became too ill to travel, another became handicapped, and, of course, one by one they began to die out.

\* \* \*

Elizabeth Holmes, upon receiving the first reunion notice, which had been forwarded by her mother, disdained attending the reunion. Nor did she ever attend any one of the reunions that followed. Her mother died shortly after that first reunion notice. The following notices were never forwarded, never returned.

No one was sure that she had ever received any of the notices. No one knew where she lived, other than the San Francisco address. No one was in touch with her. No one seemed to care.

\* \* \*

In 1992 Bill Wagner attended the reunion alone again. This year, it was in San Antonio, Texas. He had continued going each year since 1985, when Angela died. It was always great to see all the former shipmates. But he still dreaded doing it without Angela.

On the first day of the reunion, Bill spoke to Ginny Gray Blake who stood at the end of a customers' waiting line in the hotel restaurant. He arrived at the line immediately after she did. They waited to be seated.

"Hey, Ginny," he said, "I heard about Virgil. I'm so sorry."

"Thanks, Bill. And how're you doing these days?"

"Hangin' in there. You doing okay?"

"As well as could be expected. My children and grandchildren are a big help. I don't know what I'd do without them."

"I know," he said. "I depend on my little family a lot, too."

"As a matter of fact," she said, "my children encouraged me to come to this reunion, even if it had to be alone." She swallowed hard. He noticed. He said, "Shall we have lunch together?"

"Yes. Thank you."

The line moved closer to the maitre d' station.

They lunched quietly, chatting about safe subjects. Neither wanted to dwell on the loss of his or her spouse. Ginny's loss was still raw. Bill's memories of Angela were just barely beginning to fade. However, he still missed her so much.

"You have any plans for dinner tonight?" he asked.

"Not really. I'll be going on the city tour right after lunch. Not sure when we get back."

"I'm going on the same tour. Can we have dinner together after we return? I have a rental car. We could go somewhere different from hotel restaurant fare."

"That'd be nice. Thanks."

"It'll be my pleasure." And he meant it.

\* \* \*

The tour went well, riding the bus, visiting the Alamo, viewing local monuments and parks and a fire station and the city hall, and having a coffee break at the River Walk. While there, they did some shopping. They took pictures—to show their children, they said. The bus returned them to the hotel; they freshened up and met for dinner.

At dinner, in a different restaurant, Ginny said, "I really enjoyed the afternoon. I didn't think I would ever enjoy anything like this again."

Bill said, "I know exactly what you mean. . . . Do I ever!"

They looked at each other, seeming to be searching. For what, neither was quite sure.

"So," Bill said, breaking the moment, "what time you usually have breakfast? I'm an early riser myself. I wake up around five. Is six o'clock breakfast too early for you? I'd like for you to join me."

"Well, that's just a tad early. But I'd be willing to make the supreme sacrifice."

"Great. Restaurant opens somewhat later. So, I'll meet you at the coffee shop at six. Then we'll go to breakfast at the restaurant. My treat. Okay?" he asked.

"Okay."

\* \* \*

The next day, after breakfast, there was a VR Reunion meeting to attend, minutes to be read of the last previous meeting, the treasurer's report to be read, date and place for the next reunion to be determined, new officers to elect.

Ginny and Bill lunched at the hotel coffee shop, along with the Albertsons. They spent the afternoon in the Ready Room (hospitality room), chatting with other old friends from the VR days.

That evening, Ginny and Bill sat together at the banquet dinner, along with Jean Reid, Shirley and Jim Albertson, and Helen and Rob Erwin. Snapshots were passed around. New snapshots were taken. Family stories were swapped. Other entertaining stories were shared. Hilarity was at a high peak.

Bill, suddenly assuming a serious face, ventured a question to Helen: "Helen," he said, "Angie told me, before she passed away, that both she and you had puzzling links with your pasts. That you had received a gift for your newborn daughter that obviously came from the sheik—and that she, Angie, had received, anonymously, a magazine featuring the Duke's wedding. All very mysterious and bewildering."

"That's absolutely true, Bill," Helen replied. "I've never found out how Abdul knew where I was and how he seemed to know all about me!"

"So it was with Angie. Getting that magazine in the mail was so unnerving, she had said. She and the Duke had not one bit of contact since the one letter she received from him, at the end of her next flight, after meeting him." Bill shook his head with incomprehension.

"Nor did I have contact with Abdul," Helen said. "I can still see him standing at the front of his friend's house in Morocco, as the Navy car pulled away."

"I wonder if we'll ever find out how they know so much?" Bill asked no one in particular.

Helen answered, "I seriously doubt it."

\* \* \*

The fact was, both Abdul Goshen and Kurt Beckwaithe had, coincidentally, engaged the same prestigious international investigative service agency in Europe.

An uncanny connection occurred the day Abdul's lawyer and Kurt Beckwaithe had appointments at the agency's headquarters in Geneva. Beckwaithe's appointment had just been completed, and he left the director's office. Abdul's lawyer was just entering that same office. They exchanged glimpses at each other, briefly, and then went their separate ways.

The director was mildly surprised—but only mildly—that the two men requested essentially the same services: to hunt down two different women in the same Naval unit of the same time period. Apparently, his two newest clients did not know each other. *Another strange coincidence in this business,* the director said to himself.

At the outset, Abdul and Kurt were not aware of each other's search for information. Abdul tracked Helen. Kurt tracked Angela. Abdul knew *everything* about Helen, and Kurt knew *everything* about Angela.

\* \* \*

The end of the reunion came too soon, it seemed to Bill. It seemed that way to Ginny, as well. He drove her to the airport after breakfast on the day everyone departed for their homes across country. Jean Reid, however, headed for England; she had already visited her family in Arizona.

Ginny's flight left before Bill's did. He accompanied her to her departure gate. After they found seating together in the waiting area, Bill said to her, "You going to the reunion next year? I'd be pleased to see you again."

"I'm sure I'll be there," she said with a smile.

"I sincerely hope so." He seemed to hesitate when he said, "I've looked you up in the Reunion Directory. May I e-mail you some time?"

"Of course. Do that."

They stood up when her flight-loading announcement was made. He hugged her. She hugged him back. She wept, copiously onto his shoulder. He was aware of it, naturally, and he kept her within his embrace a bit longer.

"See you next year," he said into her ear.

"Oh, yes!" She pulled away to blot the tears and blow her nose.

"Goodbye, Ginny. Have a safe flight."

"Goodbye, Bill. You have a safe one, too."

As she approached the ticket taker, in a long line, he called to her, "I'm looking forward to next year!"

She smiled and waved to him. "Me, too!"

\* \* \*

Those members who are still alive, still ambulatory, and of sound mind, continue attending their reunions. Every year, the former flight attendants, who are still living and able to travel, meet together, recalling amusing, joyful, and sometimes tearful, memories. They remember that—they also flew.

# GLOSSARY

| | |
|---|---|
| AFB | Air Force Base |
| AMM | Aviation Machinist's Mate (also known as aviation mechanic, or aviation mech) |
| ATC | Air Transport Command |
| BOQ | Bachelor Officers Quarters |
| brown bagger | one who carries his lunch in a brown paper bag |
| chock | a block or wedge used for blocking movement of a wheel |
| chock-to-chock | lapse of time between take-off and landing (beginning when the chocks are removed, at departure, and ending when chocks are replaced, at destination) |
| deadheading | crew member flying as a non-participating crew member |
| deck | floor |
| deecee | D.C. (as in Washington, D.C.) |
| ditty bag | a bag for carrying small items, such as toilet articles |
| Ens.. | Ensign |
| GI | Government Issue, literally. Also an enlisted man in the army. |
| ladder | stairway |
| Lt.Cdr. | Lieutenant Commander |
| Lt.(jg) | Lieutenant (Junior Grade) |
| MAC | Military Airlift Command |
| MATS | Military Air Transport Service |
| mech | mechanic (or, machinist's mate) |
| musette bag | knapsack or tote bag |
| NAS | Naval Air Station |
| NATS | Naval Air Transport Service |
| NCO | Non-commissioned Officer |
| NROTC | Naval Reserve Officers Training Corps |
| OCS | Officer Candidate School |
| Ops | Operations (a department in a Navy squadron) |
| Pax | Patuxent River, Maryland |
| PNR | Point of No Return |
| RAF | Royal Air Force |
| R&R | Rest and Recreation |
| RON | Remain Overnight |
| scoop | as a noun, the latest information |
| SGM | Sergeant Major (highest enlisted rank in U.S. Army) |
| skeleton crew | bare-bones crew (not a full complement) |

| | |
|---|---|
| **skinny** | as a noun, the latest information |
| **St. John's** | St. John's, Newfoundland |
| **supernumerary** | a standby |
| **USAFB** | U.S. Air Force Base |
| **USN** | U..S. Navy |
| **VJ Day** | Victory in Japan Day |
| **VR** | Air Transport Squadron (heavier-than-air aircraft squadron) |
| **WAVES** | Women Accepted for Voluntary Emergency Service |
| **W/Cdr** | Wing Commander (RAF equivalent to a USN Commander) |